MIRROR, MIRROR

MIRROR, MIRROR

LAUREL HANDFIELD

A

PUBLICATION

A STREBOR BOOKS INTERNATIONAL LLC PUBLICATION
DISTRIBUTED BY SIMON & SCHUSTER, INC.

Published by

SBI

Strebor Books International LLC
P.O. Box 1370
Bowie, MD 20718
http://www.streborbooks.com

ISBN-10: 1-59309-014-5
ISBN-13: 978-1-59309-014-2

Distributed by Simon & Schuster, Inc.
1230 Avenue of the Americas
New York, NY 10020
1-800-223-2336

Cover art: © www.mariondesigns.com

First Printing February 2004
Manufactured and Printed in the United States

10 9 8 7 6 5 4 3 2 1

Also by Laurel Handfield
My Diet Starts Tomorrow

DEDICATION

To my Family, Dad, Mom, Dawn, Sharon, and Steve
Thanks for your never-ending support no matter what.
I love you guys.

ACKNOWLEDGMENTS

I would first and foremost like to thank God for allowing me to find a gift that I am able to share with others for a second time. Let's hope there's a third.

Thank you to my husband for dealing with me and my incessant chatter about every single character in every single book I have written thus far and a special thank you to my daughter who has always and will continue to be my inspiration. I love you both so very much.

Thanks to my family. They continue to support me every single day of my life.

I can't forget my friends again, Alicia Hill, Lynn Collins, and Tara Bailey. I promise I won't bore you so much with my book talks.

To Jennifer Wash, thank you for coming so see me on my book tour. I know what that meant considering you hate the Beltway, too-LOL

Thanks again to Sydney. I owe you a lot.

To those people who have inadvertently shaped the person you see before you today, I thank you. I wouldn't have changed a thing, good or bad.

To those hard-working people at Strebor. I thank you for putting the finished product together and making it look good. Thank you,

Charmaine. I truly appreciated everything you did for me. Make sure you get a raise—you deserve it.—LOL

I would like to thank Zane for even giving me another opportunity to express myself. As always, I really do appreciate it and hope we are able to work together for a long time to come.

Lastly, I would like to thank those readers who have enjoyed my books and those future readers who will enjoy my books. This is yet another one that was made for you.

God Bless,
Laurel Handfield

Never cease the struggle for personal success.
I haven't and never will.

Laurel Handfield

PROLOGUE

She felt her body fall lifeless as she writhed in tremendous pain. She attempted to take a deep breath but was unable to fill her lungs with the oxygen they so craved. She looked around and saw nothing but the luminosity of daylight radiating through a small iridescent window in the corner of the room. Brilliant, shining light filled the room to capacity. The room smelled of a disinfectant that pierced her nostrils. She could see people walking all around her aimlessly. None of them paid her any mind. The look of perplexity was apparent in their faces as they stared straight ahead while continuing their futile march. She was perspiring profusely with the tiny droplets being swallowed by her pillow. She was unable to move or speak. The only thing she could do was watch vulnerably as the other patients ambled in front of her like mummies, with each creating the same resonant sound. It wasn't a song and it wasn't a hum—it was more like a chant.

Slowly the pain throughout her body was disappearing. It was as if someone had magically cut a hole into her callused skin allowing the hurt to permeate into the atmosphere and out of her body to give her more and more strength.

CHAPTER 1

"JORDAN!!!! Coffee for Trent *now!*" Mr. Hines, her boss, yelled from the intercom he rarely used.

Jordan jerked up from her desk and immediately ran to the coffee room. She would do anything for Mr. Prescott, even if it was at the request of that ass Hines. Anything he wanted was anything he got. Especially if he wanted her in a long sleek, flowing see-through teddy just like last night.

Ahhhhh. Last night. It had been so special, so ideal. They had concluded the perfect evening at Trent's penthouse apartment where he made feral, passionate love to her all night long.

Jordan opened the top counter and reached for a coffee mug. She remembered each detail vividly. When she peered into the apartment, she saw a wildly gigantic open space mutedly lit with scented candles scattered throughout the immaculate room.

Earlier that evening they had shared a candlelit dinner at a cozy little restaurant aptly named L'Amour. It was there he donned her with a sparkling diamond bracelet from Tiffanys. The dinner of lamb, new potatoes and a vegetable medley had been delicious. When he brought her back to his place for the "dessert," she'd been more than willing to accept his love. He had opened the door and scooped her up in his arms to take her through the front gates of his kingdom as if they had just been united in holy matrimony. He delicately placed her on top of the bearskin rug in front of the blazing fireplace and kissed her softly.

Oh yes, the memory was so clear now.

Wait, no; she took the fireplace out of her gilded reverie because there was no need for one in the middle of July.

Start over.

Before Jordan could mentally redesign her vision, she heard her name being called from down the hall.

"JORDAN!"

Jordan reached into the drawer, pulled out a spoon and quickly mixed the steaming liquid in the cup. She would have to finish her fantasy when she retired for the night. Hopefully it would replace the nightmares she had had for the past few evenings. As for right now, she had to get his coffee to him pronto.

When she reached Hines' door, she tapped quietly and waited for a response. There was none so she knocked a little louder.

"Come in!" the voice boomed from behind the large oak door.

Jordan carefully placed her free hand on the doorknob and balanced the coffee in the other hand while slowly turning the brass knob. Before she knew it, an impatient Hines thrust open the door from the other side and immediately sent her plummeting into the office. She spilled the extremely hot liquid down the front of her new white J.C. Penney blouse.

Jordan winced in pain as the coffee seethed its way through the blouse and onto her skin. Hines, who was on his headset phone system, cut his eyes in disgust and said nothing to her and continued with his phone call. On the floor, Jordan looked up for Mr. Prescott. Thank goodness he was no longer in the room to witness this humiliation.

Hines walked toward his desk and grabbed some tissues. He strolled back over to her, practically shoving them in her face, all of this while still talking on the phone. She reached out for the tissues with some slowly flailing to the floor. As she bent down to pick them up, her glasses fell from her face and landed lens down in the moist section of the floor where the coffee had stained the gray carpet.

"I'm sorry. I'll get this cleaned up right away." She was on her hands and knees dabbing the wet spot with the dilapidated tissues.

"Just leave it and get me another cup," Hines said, shooing her off. His face was now a deep shade of red. This was a tremendous feat considering his dark, rich complexion.

Mr. Hines was a true jackass. Everyone in the small office thought so. That could be why he wasn't married, although he kept a picture of some butt ugly woman on his desk which they all knew wasn't his wife. According to rumors, he never got married. He did keep a bevy of women on the side. For whatever purpose she didn't know and didn't want to know. The thought sickened her to her stomach.

Hines was neither handsome nor repulsive. He was just there. She guessed him to be in his mid-forties but he had a perpetual crinkle right between his eyes that made him appear much older. He was extremely tall and his stature made him even more Goliath-like. He could be considered attractive if you didn't know him, but to Jordan there just wasn't anything physically eye-catching about him. After all, she knew him and knew him well. He was one of those men who was always right and never thought twice about telling everybody so. He was also a callous man who had no people skills whatsoever and didn't give two hoots about anyone or anything but his checkbook. That was probably another reason why he wasn't married—the whole alimony factor after the inevitable divorce. To her, it was like he was the devil incarnate.

As Jordan got up and headed toward the door to retrieve him another cup, she heard him say something behind her.

"And this time, be more careful! The cleaning of my carpet will definitely be coming out of your pay."

Jerk! she thought as she closed the door behind her.

This seemed to be the direction Jordan's life was headed. That is, until the murders took place and that changed everything.

CHAPTER 2

"Girlfriend, I don't know how you let that man treat you like that."

Jordan had hurried home in the unbelievable rush-hour traffic to tell her roommate Terry about the horrid events of the day.

"That wasn't even the worst part of it. Later on in the day, he had me go get him his lunch and his dry cleaning."

"Oh, no he didn't." Her roommate tugged at the Venetian blinds, attempting to allow the sun's rays into the gloomy room.

Jordan shook her head and held up her hand to indicate that even *that* wasn't the worst part.

"When I brought the dry cleaning back, he must've been out to lunch, so I went into his office and carefully laid the clothes down on his chair. Well, as I went to lay them down, I knocked over this vile plant that sits right in the middle of his desk. Of course the soil and water seeped right through the plastic and onto his newly cleaned jacket."

Terry let out a howl.

"Good for you. What did your asshole boss have to say to that?"

"Nothing yet because by the time he got back, I had already left for the day, but I'm sure I'll hear it tomorrow."

Jordan sighed at the mere thought of getting chastised by Hines yet again. At this point she shouldn't have cared but it was when he did it in front of everybody that embarrassed her.

She'd been at PHC Industries—named after the owners—for only three months but in that short time frame, she had managed to get in major hot water with her boss at least three times that she could recall. This whole dry cleaning thing would be the fourth. She couldn't understand why they didn't just fire her. She was no good as a secretary and she tried telling the temp service that, but they were only interested in getting their commission, so off she went. Besides, it was a job. Now only if she could keep it. Technically, she was supposed to work for two bosses, one unfortunately being Hines, and the other, a fine specimen of a man by the name of Trent Prescott. To her dismay, Mr. Prescott had gotten his own personal secretary and really never called on her for anything.

"You take so much shit from that man. I'm glad he finally got his. Now maybe he'll think twice about asking you to do all that Jeffrey the butler shit."

"I know, but what can I do? He treats everyone like this."

"Girl, stop making excuses for the man. An asshole is only as big as its owner."

Jordan knew this was an excuse but she had to come up with something as to why she allowed him to treat her this way. Bill Hines was a jerk but, on the other hand, Trent made it all worthwhile. Now, that was one good-looking man. Trent Prescott had a tawny complexion that turned this striking shade of reddish-brown when he was out in the sun for a long period of time. He was the antithesis of Hines, as opposite as opposites could get, and he could dress the heck out of anything because he had the body of Persius. Although she never saw his stomach—except in her fantasies—she could imagine no less than a six-pack underneath his cleanly pressed white shirts. He was tall, lean and every day he smelled of Dial soap with just the faintest hint of cologne. Even his nails were clean and tidy. Unlike Hines, who constantly had dirt or Lord knows what else under his fingernails, Trent kept his nails unsoiled. For some men it just came natural and he was one of those men.

Even though Jordan had only been there for a short time, she had gotten the 411 on him. In fact she had gotten it the first day she was there. Hines and Prescott were co-owners of PHC Industries and although it was a small company that dealt with financing, it was growing and seemed to be doing very well.

Trent Prescott was only forty-two years old and had been married to Jaqueline—his ex-model wife—for fifteen years and had no kids and no pets. She'd figured the no-kids situation was due more to Mrs. Rodriguez-Prescott moreso than him. Last month PHC Industries had sponsored a "Bring Your Kids to Work Day." She saw firsthand how he loved children. While Hines locked his door for the day to keep the rugrats out, Trent constantly had kids running in and out of his office all day long.

"Can't you get rid of him and just work for that fine Trent you keep drooling over?" Her roommate was always in the know of everything she did; regardless of her telling him or not.

Jordan had reached across the table to grab her fourth slice of pepperoni pizza when she met Terry's disapproving eyes.

"Actually, just the reverse. I basically just work for Hines now." She looked in the other direction; ignoring the gaze she knew was upon her.

When there was no response, she looked up at Terry.

"What?" It was really a rhetorical question because she knew exactly what.

Terry had been after her to lose weight for the past six months. Her roommate always insisted that she had a gorgeous face and if she could just manage to lose a few pounds, she'd be a knockout. Her roommate even offered to work out with her. They joined some big-named spa at a ridiculously skyrocketed price they alleged was a discount. When it came time to go, Jordan made up excuse after excuse. One of the most used ones was that she had to work late when she knew good and well she was at McDonald's downing her second cheeseburger. The most creative one came when she told Terry she twisted her ankle while walking up the two flights of stairs she alleged she did every day to get to her office. She didn't even know where the dang stairway was in that building.

Jordan smiled as she thought about that clever lie. She had limped on that ankle for four days before Terry gave up and just stopped asking. That was the last she had heard about working out. Besides, little did Terry know, she had lost some weight—twelve pounds to be exact. Her roommate probably couldn't tell because she was still wearing the same dumpy clothes she always wore. The fact of the matter was, they were loose on her, but she didn't even want to get into it like that right now. All she wanted to do was enjoy her slice of pizza in peace.

"You keep eating like that and you won't be able to fit through that door." Terry nodded toward the front door.

"What are your plans tonight?" Jordan was eager to change the subject before Terry really laid into her.

Lately, her roommate's favorite subject seemed to be her appearance.

Her roommate immediately perked up.

"Well, I've got a date with Charles again tonight and tonight I've decided to let him wax that ass." Terry grinned and slapped his backside, which made a loud clapping noise. "I might even let him suckie, suckie my little dickie tonight."

Jordan's nose furrowed in disgust. She should've been used to her gay roommate's conversations by now, but from time to time it still grossed her out to hear him talk like that.

When Jordan had seen his ad in the paper for a roommate two years ago, she didn't realize Terry was gay. The ad read plain and simple: *Single male looking for a roommate. No pets or kids.* What it should've read was: *Single gay male looking for a roommate who doesn't mind numerous men for my sexual pleasure coming in and out of a two-bedroom apartment at all hours of the night. Applicants need to be hard of hearing so as not to hear various erotic, sometimes vulgar noises coming from the bedroom. Please apply within.*

"Girl, before I forget, I'm not gonna be home tonight." He winked and blew a kiss at her.

When Jordan failed to ask why, he volunteered the unnecessary information. She was actually just thankful that she didn't have to hear Terry and his new conquest lewdly fornicating all night long. She needed to be up extra early for work the next morning.

Terry was an intelligent, good-looking gay man. He kept his body thin, but very firm. Working out almost every day had allowed him to accomplish this feat. He cared a lot when it came to his appearance, which is precisely why she couldn't understand how he did what he did with his body with all these lowlife men he claimed he was "dating." Dating for Terry was synonymous with sex. He confided in her one night telling her that a close uncle had sexually abused him and when he told his parents, they had kicked him out. That was sixteen years earlier and he hadn't spoken to either one of them since.

She sometimes felt sorry for him because even though he never really spoke on it anymore, she could tell by the occasional sadness in his eyes that it affected him more than he cared to admit.

Jordan knew he had plastic surgery, although he never admitted it and probably never would. His nose was pencil thin and his eyebrows were infinitely raised in the attention position. She also believed he had black eyeliner tattooed under his eyes. No matter the time of day, his eyes were always made up.

"I'm spending the night at Charles' and gittin' my freak on." Luckily he gave her the watered-down version of his soon-to-come illicit sexual acts.

"Have fun." She picked up another slice of pizza and brought it to her mouth, ready to bite into the pepperonis ensconced in melted cheese.

Jordan glanced up and saw Terry looking at her with knitted brows.

"Girl, lemmie do your hair. I can hook you up. That is what I do for a living, ya know."

"Oh please," Jordan began. "You're a hospital orderly and you do hair on the side. I keep telling you to open up a shop and work for yourself, but you just keep putting it off."

Terry cocked his head to the side and put his hands on his hips in his ready-to-read-somebody position.

"I would open up my own shop if you broke-down bi-atches would actually pay in money instead of food stamps like ya'll be tryin' to do."

He walked into the kitchen, laughing at his own joke.

"Besides," he yelled from the kitchen, "that orderly job pays the bills for now, but don't you worry your pretty little head over it because I don't plan to be there for too much longer! You can best believe that. I've got plans, baby."

He walked back into the room with a glass of soda. He looked at her hair again and once again changed the subject back to her. "You have beautiful, naturally curly hair and day in and day out I have to watch you wear that God-awful ponytail in that nasty - looking clippy-thing that you've had since you were nine. Let it go."

He put his glass on the table, walked over to her and yanked at the straining barrette that was holding her thick hair in place.

"Ouch!"

Once the barrette was free, with some hair she was sure, he began thumbing through her scalp with his long sinewy fingers.

"Hmmmm, just as I figured. You need a perm badly and we can throw some highlights up in there, too."

Jordan yanked her head from his fingers and stood up from the table.

"Thanks, but no thanks. I like my hair just fine."

"Whatever." He turned on his heel and walked to his room, taking a sip of soda while flipping her off. "If you ever want to de-dumpify yourself, gimme a call."

He slammed the door to his bedroom, still mumbling under his breath.

Thank goodness, Jordan thought to herself. Now she was able to eat in peace.

Jordan picked up her remaining slice of pizza and took a huge bite, washing it down with an enormous gulp of soda.

"Now this is what I'm talkin' ' bout," she said to herself. "Peace and quiet."

CHAPTER 3

"Beep, beep, beep."

Jordan reached over and slammed the snooze button on her alarm clock. She blindly reached for her eyeglasses on the nearby, unleveled nightstand. The clock read five-thirty and she knew she should be getting up; especially if she decided to try and tackle her hair today, as Terry had so tactfully suggested the night before. She already had decided she was going to do this that day, even before Terry's suggestion. But she didn't want to give him the satisfaction, so she made no mention of it.

She rolled out of bed and looked outside her tiny-latticed window. Small droplets of water hung loosely on the fire escape, indicating it had recently rained. The gloomy bulbous clouds looming above threatened more to come.

Languorously, she walked to the bathroom and began the search for her curling iron, which she had not seen in like a gazillion years. Once she found it under one of Terry's old, dusty *Vogue* magazines dating back two years, she knew it was time to clean the bathroom cabinets.

After plugging the aged contraption in on its highest setting, she retreated to the kitchen. She opened up the refrigerator and pulled out the pizza box that contained the last two slices. After popping them into the microwave, she reached back into the refrigerator and grabbed the rest of the soda she hadn't finished the night before. She took a swig straight from the bottle and relished every syrupy gulp.

"I really need to cut out all of the junk food," she said to herself as she passed the full-length mirror on the way to the bathroom for a hot shower.

After her shower Jordan decided this would be the perfect time to weigh herself. No, wait, she had to dry herself off first. The drops of water would probably add another five pounds.

After completely drying off, she pulled the scale out from under the sink and was then ready to step on. No, wait. She reached up to her head and flipped off the shower cap and then proceeded to take off her bracelet, her necklace and her earrings. Now she was ready. She stepped up on the scale with her eyes closed. When she looked down, she almost fell backward. She couldn't believe it. She somehow had managed to lose another pound. She wasn't really on a diet and she hadn't been watching her weight at all. Then again, since starting this job, she hadn't been eating as much. Oh well, she wasn't complaining. Go 'head, girl.

Jordan stepped off the scale and reached for the blazing-hot curling iron. She grabbed a small section of curly hair and began straightening it, beginning at the crown and slowly sliding it down to the end of the single piece of hair where she then curled it under. She did this all the way around until each piece was straight and only bent at the bottom; ridding her of her natural curl. When she looked in the mirror at the finished product, she thought it looked pretty damn good.

Since it was Friday and dress-down day, she opted to wear a pair of khaki pants and another white button-down blouse she got at Penney's at a two-for-one.

She even put on a smidgen of lip gloss.

Yup, she looked pretty good, if she should say so. Good enough to even catch Mr. Prescott's eye. It's just too bad that Terry wasn't home to see her looking all glamorous. This would've shut him up for a while.

By the time she was ready to go, it had begun to rain steadily. She went to the closet for her umbrella but it wasn't there. She went to Terry's room and knocked. She knew he wasn't home, but out of habit she knocked anyway. Besides, it's better to be safe than sorry and she wasn't trying to walk in on anything he might've been doing in there.

Jordan opened the door and walked in. His room was like a dark, moist cave swelled with inscrutability. The sheets on his bed were crumpled and had the air of sex attached to every wrinkle. He even had women's lingerie strewn all over the place.

She just wanted to find what she had come for and get out of there without incident. Her umbrella was nowhere in sight, but there was one last place to check. She turned toward the closet where there was a light illuminating from the bottom crack of the door. She was almost afraid of what was in there. Terry had "eccentric" pastimes and the evidence of those hobbies might come flying out of that closet if she dared to open it up and cross over to the dark side. She turned the knob and was half relieved to find that it was locked.

Never mind; she had to go. If she ran to the bus stop, it probably wouldn't be that bad anyway.

Jordan briskly retreated out of his room and shut the door to Terry Land. She hurried over to the front door, stumbling over some unknown obstruction sitting in the middle of the floor. Walking out the front door and locking it behind her, she scurried off into the rain to the bus stop.

By the time she reached the stop, she was out of breath. She had no mirror to see her reflection, but by the piece of hair that hung in her eyes, it was evident that it might have fallen a bit.

"Better get used to it. It's supposed to rain all week."

Jordan looked over her left shoulder and saw an elderly woman looking straight up at the sky. She then turned and looked over her right shoulder to see if there was someone else standing there. There was no one.

Apparently, she was talking to her. The old woman had been coming to the bus stop every day for the past three months and had never uttered a word to her; just sort of watched her all the time in silence.

Jordan peered over her left shoulder as she responded to the woman. "That stinks."

"We actually need the rain. Everything needs to grow and although it may be an inconvenience for us, it's great for the trees, flowers and grass." The elderly lady was still looking up toward the clouds.

"Mmmmm, hmmmmm," was all Jordan said.

Maybe she wasn't talking to her. She could be one of those crazy old ladies that just liked to ramble on and on.

"Never discount the rain. It has a purpose. It may not suit your purpose but it has its purpose regardless."

The old lady switched her gaze from the murky sky to her. She smiled a wide, near toothless grin. "Just remember that, dear."

Yeah, whatever.

The bus came putt-putting from around the corner, squeaking to a halt in front of the two women who were patiently standing under the bus stop canopy.

"In all these years, they still haven't gotten the brakes fixed on this thing. It's not old age that's gonna kill me; it's this bus." The woman cackled at her own comment and stepped up onto the broke-down vehicle.

✳✳✳

When Jordan reached her office building, she ran to the elevator doors that stood open. She stepped in and got uncanny stares from the mass of people already there waiting. As she stood up front, she heard giggling and whispering in back of her. When the full elevator closed, she was horrified at the reflection that stared back at her in the shiny silver doors. Her beautifully styled hair looked like a complete Afro with absolutely no curl and what's worse, it had droplets of rain scattered throughout. The makeup she attempted to wear was now in smears on her face. She looked past her reflection and saw the gigglers and whisperers were pointing at her and laughing.

She closed her eyes and thanked the stars that her desk was only on the second floor. When the elevator finally read two, it took forever for the doors to open. Once they did, she shot out like a torpedo aiming for its path of destruction.

She reached her desk and immediately pressed the little button on her computer to turn it on. Plopping down the bag she carried to work every day, she attempted to do a fast retreat to the bathroom for some necessary revitalizing. Mere seconds later, she heard her name being bellowed by Mr. Hines on the other side of his door.

"Jooooooooooordannnnnn!"

Was he friggin' listening for her?

Jordan thought about acting like she hadn't heard his hollered-out screech until his office door thrust open and there he stood with that crinkle between his brows. He looked from her hair to her, having no idea what to say.

That didn't last long.

"I need you to call the Donnelly Company right away," he barked at her, obviously ignoring her hair emergency. He then reached for her favorite pen from her desk. She knew she would never see it again.

She made sure he saw her looking at her watch to indicate that yes, she was early and that yes, technically she wasn't on the clock. It was only eight twenty-three.

Didn't matter.

"And once you have them on the phone, give me a holler. Prescott should be here any minute for our conference call so do it now, please."

She didn't even have two minutes to run to the bathroom to fix her hair and makeup and now that she knew Mr. Prescott was coming, she needed to do it and do it quickly.

Jordan sat back down behind her desk and opened her top right-hand drawer to reach for her compact mirror. Damn, damn, damn. She forgot she had taken it home the previous week. Oh well, she would just have to wing it. Reaching into her purse, she pulled out a brush and began tugging at the fuzzy formation on top of her head.

"Did you get them on the line yet?" Hines yelled from behind his door.

She looked at the intercom on her desk, desperately trying to figure out why in the hell she had this thing seeing as he never used it.

Now that ass could see from his office that she wasn't on the line yet.

Without saying a word, she picked up the phone and leafed through the antiquated paper-flip Rolodex at the same time.

Didn't most companies use computer organizers in this day and age?

She balanced the phone on her shoulder while using her right hand to brush her bird's nest and her left hand to dial. Once she reached the Donnelly Company, she transferred the call directly to 248, her boss' extension, and hung up. She got up, and without delay, headed for the bathroom. But it was too late. Mr. Prescott was whistling down the hall with that impeccable stroll of his.

Defeated, she quietly plopped down into her seat.

Well, there's nothing I can do now, she thought to herself. Before she knew it, her someday-future-husband-once-he-gets-a-divorce-from-his-wife was standing in front of her across her desk.

"Well, good morning. Rain got you, too, huh?" He was actually beaming at her.

Jordan looked up at him and saw he was a wet mess from head to toe. He had drops of water in his hair, too, as she was sure she still had in hers.

"Is Billy in already?" He looked back at the closed office door.

"Yes. He said to go right in." She grinned as if she were a grade-school girl telling her best friend about the boy she liked in math class.

"Thank you, ma'am," he said in a joking manner as he walked toward the door. He stopped suddenly when he put his hand on the doorknob to enter.

"By the way, you should wear your hair out more often. It looks nice, minus some of that terrible rain."

He turned the knob and walked into hell's fire.

Almost knocking over a cup full of pencils, she jerked up from her desk and headed for the ladies room. Maybe her hair wasn't that bad after all.

Jordan looked into the smudged mirror in the ladies room and actually it wasn't that bad. It was a little puffy from the rain but that was it. You could still see that it had some style to it.

Maybe I'll let Terry do my hair tonight, she thought as she studied her reflection. After all, how many times does it rain two days in a row?

CHAPTER 4

"It's about freakin' time." Terry slopped a heap of Dark and Lovely relaxer onto the crown of her head.

The rain was coming down much harder than earlier in the day and made a loud hostile noise on the roof.

Terry could hook anyone up with a perm but it was a surefire guarantee that you came out of there with burns all up and down your scalp.

"You're gonna let me clip those ends, too, right?" He picked up the scissors and began cutting into air.

"Just do what you have to do to make it look good."

"You're doing this all for that fine Prescott, aren't you?" He parted her hair with a fine-tooth comb and carelessly slapped on more perm. "Too bad he's married. If you'd fix yourself up a little, put some makeup on, keep your hair done, get some new clothes and maybe lose…"

The sound of thunder boomed through the tiny apartment immediately followed by nature's light fluorescing the faintly lit room like a strobe light.

"I get the message." She was beginning to get disconcerted at the mere mention of her losing weight again. He was about to start in on the weight thing and she wasn't having it.

"Actually, it looks as though you've lost some of your big bountiful bodacious butt," he said matter-of-factly.

Jordan wasn't going to fall for that trick. He just wanted to engage her in a weight conversation with the faux compliment. She had taken Psych-101 in college, too.

"Really, it looks like it. You wanna be careful and not lose too much of it though. You know how brothas hate a skinny behind. You wanna keep a little junk in that trunk," he said, rubbing his own posterior. "This, I know."

Plop. More perm slapped on her hair.

"Regardless, I think you're beautiful anyway." He leaned down to kiss her right cheek.

Jordan started to smile. He got her on that one. He could be such a corny jerk at times.

Terry stepped from behind her and was now facing her with his hand on his hips and a sly smile on his face. Just from his stance, she could tell that he was about to ruin the moment. Whenever he put his hands on his hips he had something to say and usually it was something she didn't care to hear. Any minute now, words she didn't want to hear would come out of those parted lips of his.

Jordan reached around him and his gaze and grabbed the metal comb sitting on the kitchen table.

"Just finish my hair, puh-leese." She thrust the comb in his face.

"Shows what you know." He grabbed it from her hands and smacked it back down onto the table. "This comb is for straightening."

"So if I'm getting a perm, what do I need the comb for?"

He raised an eyebrow.

"Hmmmph. Girl, no offense, but I need backup just in case."

He grabbed at her hair and pulled his hands back quickly, as if he had just received an electrical shock.

"Owwwww! See what I mean?"

Ha, ha, very funny. ·

He could've ended the conversation on the beautiful comment but nooooooo…

Jordan smiled at him.

Although he teased her constantly, he could be such an angel sometimes.

❋❋❋

The next day Jordan walked into the office with her "new look." The night before, Terry relaxed her hair ever so slightly, enhancing its natural curl. He trimmed it an inch to give it more shape and body. He put some of his makeup on her face, and not the cheap stuff either. Terry had that expensive makeup for his men. He spent time showing her how to pluck her eyebrows and how to do things like wear false eyelashes and apply mascara without looking like a rabid raccoon. She nipped it in the bud when he attempted to strategically place a penciled-in mole on her face for the Cindy Crawford look. Then and there she had to remind him that she wasn't dressing up in drag and told him to take it down a notch or two. Apart from that, he had done an excellent job. He even talked her into wearing the contact lenses she had bought a long time ago but never wore. She had to check the expiration date to make sure they were still good. It had been that long.

Even though it was raining, her hair was laid in its natural, soft curl and kept its style. Since her hair was naturally curly—thanks to her Dominican mother, God rest her soul—Terry showed her that a mild relaxer would help keep the curl natural. If applied properly it would be manageable. Even the old lady at the bus stop didn't recognize her right away. She had to take a closer look to realize that it was her.

"With all that goo on your face, I almost didn't recognize you." She kept a straight face and stared directly at her without a blink.

"Your hair actually reminds me of my French poodle I had as a young girl," the old woman had told her.

Terry even went as far as to let her borrow some of his "straight clothes." She chose this pretty floral skirt and short-sleeved white blouse from one of those ritzy boutiques rather than Penney's. Now that she lost a few pounds, she could fit into his clothes. They were a little snug but according to Terry, it was perfect.

Everyone seemed to notice the change in her appearance, including the mailroom guys on the bottom floor, but they hit on every woman that stood upright and breathed oxygen so that didn't really count.

After passing everyone in her office and getting the responses she had hoped for, she reached her desk and sat down. The first thing she did was pull out the mirror she brought from home out of her bag. She studied her reflection again. She couldn't believe the miracle Terry had pulled off. Not only did she look presentable but she looked good. She made a mental note to go home to practice the art of putting on makeup that night since Terry informed her that he would be spending the night at Dick's.

No comment on that one.

Jordan patted down her hair one more time and then put the mirror back into her bag and placed it under her desk. When she looked up, her coworker Gerald was standing at her desk looking down her blouse and making no secrets of it either.

She looked up at him, trying to convey her annoyance. "Can I help you?"

"What a coincidence. I was just about to ask you the same question." He winked not at her, but at her boobs, which he was still conspicuously leering at.

Gerald was her buddy in the accounting department. He was funny as hell but sometimes he got on her nerves. He was always around and seemed to know everybody's business. He was that brotha at work that was one sick day away from being fired. As a matter of fact, rumor had it that he had been fired before, but was

26

somehow rehired due to some sort of blackmail he had on one of the bosses. Now that was hard to believe but no one knew what the real deal was, and he wasn't about to disclose information that made him the talk of the office. It was his job to talk about everyone else. Whenever asked about it, he would just give his usual tired wink and smile and say, "Connections, baby, connections."

"So what are you all dolled up for?" He walked around her desk and placed his posterior on the edge so that his manhood was practically in her face.

"What are you talking about?" She ignored the propinquity of his genitalia and reached around him to turn on her computer.

"Oh, c'mon. The hair, the makeup and the new clothes? If I had to see that white blouse one more time, I was gonna rip that thing off and use it as toilet paper." He stood up to provide her with the lovely visual to his uncouth comment.

Wow, she couldn't believe that he, of all people, didn't have a woman.

"Who told you to check out my clothes anyway?"

"Hey, hey, don't get mad. I was just being observant."

She looked up at him and cut her eyes in disgust.

"Yeah okay. Whatever you say."

He put his thumb and index finger on his chin and began to rub.

"You do know you look good. It even looks like you lost some weight."

She didn't care about his opinion. There was only one person she was trying to impress—Trent—and he wasn't even in the office yet. He'd better see her before her makeup wore off because she didn't bring any backup with her.

"Hiney isn't coming in today. Bet you didn't know that." Gerald thrust out his chest with pride.

Gerald and the whole department called her boss Hiney because he was such an ass.

"He mentioned something about it." She felt as though she had to lie to him in order to bust his bubble. She wasn't about to give him the satisfaction that he so craved when he knew something somebody else didn't.

It must've worked because he looked shocked that she would know this. Now she would never find out why he wasn't coming in, but it really didn't matter. Just the fact that she wouldn't have to deal with Hines' crap today and being able to shoot down Gerald at the same time was enough for her. But did that mean that Mr. Prescott wasn't coming in either? That would just be her luck. All dressed up and no place to go, and no one to see for that matter.

Jordan wasn't able to wait to find out if Gerald would "volunteer" information on Mr. Prescott so she relented and asked. In this case, it was necessary.

"So does that mean that Mr. Prescott isn't coming in either?"

"Oh, he's here already. As a matter of fact, he's in your boss' office right now. He'll be working there for the day since his computer's down."

She looked to the door in astonishment. He was already here? He was sitting on the other side of that door, probably with his feet propped up on the desk and leaning back in the leather chair, casually talking on the phone to one of his business partners.

Gerald perked up again.

"You didn't know that?" he asked, smiling.

No getting around this one so she just gave it to him.

"No, Gerald, I didn't know that one. You got me."

"Dang, girl, you need to keep up around here." He started walking away with smug satisfaction written all over his face. "Oh, and his secretary Charlotte should be coming down and taking care of him." He winked a you-know-what-that-means-wink. "You really shouldn't have to worry about him bugging you too much." He walked away still snickering.

Jordan sometimes felt sorry for Gerald. He thrived on the attention he got around the office, which was mostly negative. If he didn't have a problem with the fact that half the office wanted to kick his ass, including the women, then why should she?

Charlotte, huh?

Charlotte was Trent's personal secretary. To Jordan, she was kind of dowdy-looking. She had nerve, but if she could say Charlotte was plain, then she must be pretty bad. She was by no means unattractive though. In fact, she had one distinctive feature—her blue eyes. This was the first black woman she had seen with such piercing blue eyes. Haunting almost. Jordan heard she had been Mr. Prescott's secretary since day one, but no one on the second floor really saw her too much. She just kept to herself and did her job. That was exactly how it should've been around there. In actuality, you could probably describe her as Jordan to the fifth power when it came to the social department. Jordan preferred to keep to herself and aside from Gerald, she really didn't talk to too many people in the office.

So Trent was not only already there, he would be working in close quarters with her all day?

Should she go knock on the door and say good morning or should she just wait for him to come out? Maybe she should just head into the office and pretend that she didn't know he was working there for the day. Yeah, that would be good. She could pretend she needed a file or something and walk right in. Upon seeing him she could put her hand to her chest and act surprised, in a coy sort of way. Sounded like a plan, but before she had a chance to put her plan in motion, her intercom beeped and over the speaker came his voice. A beautiful, deep melodic voice that sounded like creamy dark chocolate syrup being spread all over her body from head to toe, engulfing her breasts, then slowly sliding down her body like a smoldering volcano on a mountainside toward her...

"Jordan?"

Her thoughts were interrupted.

How should she answer? Should she sound surprised that there was a voice coming over her intercom that was not her boss'? Should she try to sound sexy? Or maybe upbeat?

Which voice to use?

"Jordan, are you there?" the smoldering voice said again.

She'd better decide.

"Good morning, Mr. Prescott."

That was good. By saying his name it made it sound as though she was well on top of her job and knew that he was going to be in Hines' office.

The shrill in her tone could've been different though.

"Good morning. Could you come in here, please?"

She pressed the intercom button again.

"I'll be right in," she said, more sure of herself this time.

Jordan frantically reached down into her bag and pulled out the mirror. She realized she would have to do a full body check instead and this mirror wasn't big enough. She didn't have time to run to the ladies room so she stood up and ran the mirror down her body, front and back, trying to find the slightest imperfection. It was no use; she couldn't see jack.

Jordan accidentally slammed the petite pocket mirror down on her desk, nearly shattering it into tiny pieces. She walked from behind her desk and almost tripped on the leg of her chair but caught herself before disaster struck. She gained her composure and picked up the mirror once more to look at her hair and makeup.

Still in place. She was good.

Jordan sauntered up to the door. After she patted down the front of her skirt for invisible lint—you could never be too sure—she turned the knob and hesitantly opened the door.

There was Mr. Prescott on the phone. He sat at Hines' huge cherrywood desk but he was not alone. His wife, Jacqueline, was sitting across from him. Once he saw her standing at the door, he motioned for her to come in with his free hand. His wife slowly turned and looked her up and down, then turned back to her husband who was just finishing his call with the party on the other end.

"Jordan, could you hand-deliver these reports to Charlotte on the fourth floor? She should've gotten them an hour ago but I completely forgot."

She reached across the desk and grabbed the reports from his hands and accidentally brushed his fingers.

"You remember my wife, Jacquie, don't you?" He smiled across the desk at his wife.

Jordan looked down at the stunning woman sitting in the chair in her no-doubt expensive navy-colored suit with her matching shoes and her posh-style purse attached to her slender hip.

Too slender, if you were to ask her.

Meow.

Yeah, she remembered her all right.

Jacquie, as Mr. Prescott so affectionately called her, smelled of Alchimie by Rochas perfume.

She had learned quite a bit about colognes and perfumes from Terry, who, when dressed in drag, used the very same expensive scent himself.

Her jet-black hair was pulled back in a tight bun and held together with gold bobby pins, probably 14K gold.

Meow.

"Yes. We've met before." She positioned her purse from one side to the other.

What did she think, she was planning to rip her off?

When Jordan didn't move, Trent reiterated that he needed Charlotte to get the reports she was now holding in her hands—right away.

"Oh, right. I'll walk them up right now." She hastily turned for a quick retreat.

"Would you be a dear and get me a cup of coffee from your kitchen while you're at it?" Mrs. Rodriguez-Prescott said before she could exit.

Her kitchen?

"Hon, she's not that kind of secretary. She doesn't do that. Besides, the break room is right down the hall. Just go get yourself a cup." Trent attempted to come to her rescue from the beast, but the beast wouldn't back down.

"I'm sure she doesn't mind." She waved her manicured hand in the air completely dismissing her and her husband's defense. "I like cream and sugar. Thanks."

She turned back to her husband across the desk, who apparently had no more aid for her because he was now dialing the phone.

Jordan walked out of the office in near tears. She couldn't stand that woman. If she wanted coffee, she would get her some coffee. She hoped she liked cream and sugar seasoned with a little spit.

Meow!

CHAPTER 5

"Wanna go to lunch today?"

Jordan looked up at a grinning Gerald.

"No."

"Whoa, what's your problem? It must be that time of the month again."

She was in no mood for his inane sarcasm so she opted to say nothing and just hoped that he would go away. But, of course, he didn't.

"Lunch is on me. Besides, I know this hidden little Italian restaurant that no one knows about and only the big bosses go to. It's kind of far but since Hiney isn't here, we can take as long as we want."

Jordan really wanted to get out of the office and a long lunch just might do it. Besides, she needed a break from these people.

"What about Mr. Prescott? He's still here." The sheer mention of his name escaping her lips sent chills down her spine.

"What about him? Like he really cares."

Jordan thought for a moment. Mr. Prescott really was the type that didn't pay you any mind as long as you got your work done. Besides, he hadn't come out of that office since escorting his wife to the elevators earlier that morning.

"Okay, but let me at least tell him I'm going."

"I'll wait for you downstairs," Gerald said as he strolled toward the elevators. "Just hurry up. I'm starving."

Jordan got up from her desk and tapped on her boss' door.

"Come in."

She opened the door and walked in. Mr. Prescott sat at the over-sized desk with his head leaned against the back of the chair. His feet were propped up on the desk just as she imagined. He looked up into the heavens as if doing some profound thinking. The incoming sun from the large window behind him formed a light that seemed to adorn his being. When he came down from whichever cloud averted his attention, he focused on her standing in the doorway and smiled one of his sexy, but self-effacing smiles.

"Ah, Jordan, come in. What can I do for you?"

"I'm sorry to bother you. I just wanted to let you know that I'm going to lunch now."

He looked surprised and shrugged his shoulders in indifference.

"That's fine. Take your time. You didn't have to let me know, but it's nice that you did."

This was really awkward for her. Now what?

"Okay, well, I'm going." She turned to walk out of the door.

"Oh, wait a minute!" His booming request surprised her, making her jump.

She turned around and saw him motioning for her to come back in with one hand while typing something with the other.

"I have been having problems in Word. For the life of me I can't get this thing to print out correctly. Every time I hit 'print,' it gives me some sort of error message."

He spoke every single syllable with an air of confidence that she had never witnessed before. It was as if he had his own tone to the English language that no other mortal was privy to.

"Oh, his computer is weird." She walked closer to him.

He got up from the leather chair and pulled it back for her to sit. She sat down and started to fidget with his keys. She had to constantly do this for Mr. Hines in the past until he just gave up and started sending her the information that needed printing. That man hadn't printed anything on his own for a couple of months.

"It's this key right here." She pointed to the print key. "I think it's defective, so what you'll need to do is hit the F2 key along with the control button and then it will give you the option to print. Once it does, just hit 'OK' and enter. Then it should print for you."

After her explanation, she turned around to see him leaning directly behind her with one hand on the back of the chair and the other hand on the edge of the desk; creating an almost prison-like formation with his arms.

"Well, that's good to know for the next time." He looked directly into her eyes. For a split second they just looked at each other in silence. She waited for him to say something. She didn't know what *he* was waiting for.

Jordan took a deep breath and inhaled his beguiling aroma of soap and cologne. This was the closest she had ever been to him and she liked it, plus he smelled so good. He wore a mild yet very expensive cologne. She recognized that scent from Terry, too.

In an instant, he backed up from the chair to let her out of the prison of love that had encompassed her just moments before.

She took that as her cue and pushed the chair back from the desk and stood up, ready to make her exit.

"I guess I'll be going now but I won't be long, if you need anything." She surprised herself with her tone that could've had sexual connotations attached to it.

"No, I should be okay for a while. Just don't be gone too long." He bit his lower lip and winked at her.

Could he possibly be flirting with her, too?

As she started to walk out the door he called to her again.

"Oh, before you go to lunch, could you call Charlotte down for me, please?"

Jordan frowned and nodded. Disappointed, she said, "Okay,"

while still walking toward the door trying to make her getaway.

"By the way, you look very good today."

This stopped her in her tracks and she turned back to him, still watching. She tried to hide her surprise at his last comment and smile sexily, but she could feel that ten-year-old giddy smile on her face beginning to form.

"Thanks." She was eager to get out of there before she completely ruined it.

"Very nice," he repeated. This time his voice was an octave lower.

She turned and hastily walked out of the office with "the walk" that Terry had taught her.

As she shut the door behind her, a feeling of elation took over. She couldn't believe that she actually flirted with Mr. Prescott and had done it so well. Terry would've been so proud.

✹✹✹

"Girl, I gotta get a new job. I'm so tired of this shit I don't know what to do." Gerald took a bite of his cheese, meat and pasta goo. It was supposed to be lasagna but looked nothing like it.

The restaurant Gerald chose was like every other Italian restaurant she'd been in. It was a small bistro with the clichéd red and white-checkered tablecloths and a single flower placed in a plastic vase with a protracted neck at the core of the table.

He looked down at her plate and *tsk'ed.*

"How the hell you gonna come to the finest Italian restaurant in this whole area and get a salad? I mean this shit was in *The Times* as not one of the best but *the* best restaurant in town and here you go eating a salad. Who you trying to be cute for? It's only me; not your boy Prescott."

Jordan looked up from her salad at the mention of his name. Why in the hell would he mention *his* name, of all people? No one knew that she was attracted to him. She hadn't told not one of those nosy, gossiping, in-everybody's-business coworkers. Especially him.

"What? Why would you mention him?"

"I may be ig'nant but I ain't stupid. I've seen you look at him and get flustered every time you see him." He stared at her while shoveling in another bite of his goo. "That's what all this is about, isn't it?" He motioned his fork up and down at her outfit from across the table. "I mean, c'mon, don't get me wrong. You look good and all but you yourself don't give a horse's ass about your appearance unless it's for *somebody* and my guess is it's him."

Jordan had nothing to say. What could she say? He was dead-on and if she even attempted to protest, it would end up coming out like a big fat lie anyway. So she remained reticent and admitted to nothing.

"Besides, girl, you gonna hafta wait in line. Somebody else already has claims on that."

Jordan already knew nothing could ever happen because of his wife so she continued to ignore his incessant gossip.

"And it ain't just his wife either." He consumed his last piece of pasta by shoveling it all into his mouth at once, with sauce escaping and dripping onto his shirt in one large blob.

Jordan looked from his shirt to him in complete bewilderment.

Now what was he talking about?

"You idiot. What are you talking about now?" She reached across the table for the pepper.

She could see why no one in the office paid him any mind. She sometimes wondered what it was that kept her so tolerant of him.

"Don't tell me you don't know." He put his fork down and sat back in the chair. He had that smug look on his face.

This was no time for his games and she was not in the mood.

"Know what?" She sighed.

"You mean to tell me, you work with him and you don't know what's going on up in that place. You can't be that blind."

"Know what?" she repeated, only angrier this time.

He'd better talk and talk soon or she was gonna reach over this table and do something beyond her control.

"Him and Charlotte," he confessed.

He looked for some inkling in her face to indicate she knew what the hell he was talking about.

He wasn't gonna find that here.

"*What?* Mr. Prescott and Charlotte?" This was so unbelievable to her. "Oh, come on now. That's the worst rumor I've ever heard in this place."

"You really didn't know, did you?" He took a swig of water, as if to wash down the contemptible lie that escaped his lips seconds before. "This has been going on for at least six months. Not just that, she was supposedly pregnant by him, but he made her get rid of it."

The constant vernacular he used grated her nerves. It made him sound so ignorant, which she knew him not to be.

"I can't even believe you're repeating this one. You should've just kept this to yourself."

Nervously, she laughed. This had to be a rumor. It just had to be.

"No, seriously. Mrs. Prescott found out and threatened him *and* her. That's why the Mrs. is up in there all day long. To keep an eye on his ass."

"Whatever."

"Yeah, whatever. Don't believe me then."

Personally, she just wanted him to drop the subject, which he unfortunately did.

"Okay, if you're not interested in him, why not go out with me on Friday?" He didn't look up from his plate.

This amused her. She started laughing out loud. Her and Gerald? Wasn't going to happen.

When she didn't answer, he asked again.

"Oh, come on," he said suppliantly. "We could go out to the

movies or to dinner or something. You know, it wouldn't be like a date or anything. We could just hang out."

She continued laughing but eventually contained it to a small giggle. When she looked at him this time, she saw that he wasn't amused.

Ohmigod. He was serious. She didn't know how to respond to this. She didn't want to be rude; even though she had already laughed in his face twice. Who knew he was serious? Gerald was definitely not her type. Although he could be considered *cute-ish*, in a court jester sort of way, he just had too many scams going on for her. He frequently told her about all the women he was dating. It wasn't favorable information either. He once told her that he dumped a woman because she had refused to pay his way for a seven-day cruise they had planned together.

Jordan still didn't know if she believed that one but, then again, it was Gerald.

He was that person that complained every day about the job and how he wanted to get out, but never did anything to rectify the situation. He tried selling ladies clothes in the office one day, in hopes of starting his own "bidness" as he so eloquently put it. When no one bought anything from "Gerald the Sheister," that business closed down quickly, never to return.

She had never thought about him like that—ever. Now he was sitting across from her asking her the question she'd never thought she would hear from his lips.

Actually "hoped" was a better word.

"I'd like to. Really. It's just that…" she began.

"Girl, please, I wasn't serious. Don't nobody want you." He cleared his throat uneasily and went back to sipping his water.

It was settled for now, but she knew he would eventually ask her out again. They always did. At least now she knew and had to be prepared for next time. She didn't have time for tie-ups when Mr. Prescott was the man she had her eye on.

Him and Charlotte? Now that was funny.

***

An hour later when they had finished lunch, Gerald grabbed the check and offered to pay. Normally she would've accepted but not anymore. She didn't want to give him the wrong idea. They split the tab.

As they got up to leave, he stopped suddenly and peered across the room to another table. She discreetly turned her head and tracked his eyes to the back of the crowded restaurant. She saw what he must've been looking at. There was Hines with Mrs. Prescott in a booth way in the back.

There was a large woman sitting in a small Hepplewhite at a table near theirs. She was partially obstructing the view, but it unquestionably was Hines and Mrs. Prescott.

What in the hell were they doing there and together at that?

She waited for Gerald to say something smart-assed, but he didn't flinch. He put the tip on the table and turned to walk out.

"You ready?" He reached across the table and retrieved an extra dollar he had left for the tip.

"Ready?" he asked again. Once more he glanced toward the back of the restaurant.

Gerald had to have seen them. She didn't get it. This was the type of gossip he lived for. Seeing the boss with another boss' wife? He could've talked about this until five o'clock so he wouldn't have to work for the rest of the day. He could've been the hero of the office with this news.

Maybe he was looking at something else in the restaurant. After all, it was crowded. He could've been admiring the Hepplewhite woman.

When they got to his car, he reached ahead of her and opened the door. Damn, she wanted to open it herself. As simple a gesture as opening a door for someone, she still had to make sure he got the message that she wasn't interested. When she looked over at him, she saw that he wasn't even there. Not mentally anyway. He had an unreadable look on his face. His mind, no doubt, was elsewhere.

What the heck was his problem? Now this was one odd guy.

CHAPTER 6

"Giiiiiiiiirl, you still look good." Terry was out of breath upon Jordan's arrival home. He was doing his daily aerobics routine, jumping up and down in this ridiculous purple and black pinstriped leotard.

"Makeup ran a little bit," he said between gasps of air, "but you still all that."

Jordan passed the mirror and saw her reflection. Her hair was still neatly styled on her head. Terry was right. Her makeup had run a bit, but it still looked much better than on any day she had tried to do it herself. She had Terry to thank for all this. This had been the best day she'd had in that office ever since... actually, this had been the best day in that office ever—period.

She watched him stretch his body to the left, then to the right.

"And did you see your man?" He began jumping in unison with the buxom blond on the videotape.

The thought of Mr. Prescott made her smile again.

When she didn't answer right away, he stopped jumping around and raised his brow and looked at her questioningly.

"You did see your man, didn't you? I take it all went well?"

Her smile became broader. She couldn't contain herself. This day had gone better than she could've ever imagined. And she had a very vivid imagination.

"I saw him and even flirted with him a little bit. You would've been so proud of me."

Terry let out a loud scream and ran over to her and hugged her tightly. Sweat dripping and all.

"I knew you could do it. You really look-ded good with your fly self."

He walked over to the other side of the room and plopped his sweaty rear end into the recliner.

"What exactly does that company do anyway?" He tilted his head, waiting for an answer.

Why was he asking this? What difference did it make to her story? This threw her off for a moment.

"I don't know. They're financial consultants for larger firms. Who cares? I just know they have a lot of companies trying to buy them out for a lot of money." She looked at him impatiently. "Now, can I get back to my story, please?"

"Okay, okay." He was now back on track. "Tell me everything and I mean *everything*. Leave nothing out."

He leaned back in the plush chair, making himself more comfortable. Then he crossed his legs. First, right over left, then left over right. Once he stopped fidgeting, she knew he was in position to hear her story.

"Anyway, it really wasn't anything drastic." She didn't want him to expect too much; even though for her it was a lot. "But he did notice that my hair was done and made a comment on it."

He squeezed his eyes tight and scrunched his face in excitement.

"I'm sure he checked out my butt when I was walking away. Plus, when I was going to lunch, he said, get this…" She paused for a moment with anticipation in her face. She wanted to keep him in suspense and it was working. Her roommate was now sitting on the edge of the chair, awaiting what words her lips would now speak.

"Get this," she repeated for more of an effect. "He had said something like 'don't take too long for lunch.' You know, implying that he would miss me. And my comeback was something like 'if you need anything, just let me know.'" She stopped dead with her arms open, awaiting Terry's reaction.

His face dropped and he looked at her with confusion in his eyes. "Huh? I don't get it?"

"I said to him," she stated, now getting impatient, "'if you need anything, just let me know.'" This time she spoke exactly as she said it in the office with the whole flirty, sexual thing.

"Ohhhhhhh, I get it. 'If you need *anything.*'" He repeated her words but, for some reason, it sounded sexier coming out of his mouth.

"But wait." She held up her hand. "Then, I sauntered out of the office and that's when he told me that I looked good. Then he said 'very good.'"

She stood speechless with her mouth gaped, again anticipating his reaction.

He snapped his fingers. "Giiiiiirl. You got 'em."

He got up from the couch and lunged at her to give her a hug, practically knocking her over. He pulled back and his face got somber for a moment as he looked at her with bogus tears in his eyes.

"I've taught you so well. My baby girl is now all growed-up."

She pushed him off of her.

"You are so stupid." His madcap sense of humor made her laugh. This had truly been a good day for her.

"You know…" he began.

Uh-oh, this could only mean one thing. He was taking the "look at the flip side of things" again. Hands on hips and all. He always did that. He was the master at playing devil's advocate; probably better than the devil himself.

"It was all fun and games in the beginning, but do you realize that he's a married man and it sounds like you're serious about him."

He walked over to the television set and flipped out the exercise tape.

"I know we've kidded around, but are you sure this is what you want?"

There it went. Day ruined.

"Oh, I see. You were helping me in the beginning and now that it looks like he's actually interested, you're throwing this in my face."

"Yeah, but I didn't really think you could get him."

"Gee, thanks."

"I didn't mean it like that. I'm just saying, screwing around with married men could lead to trouble. Believe me, I know. I just don't want you to make any mistakes that you may regret."

Jordan didn't want to have this conversation with him. Not now. She knew Mr. Prescott was married and she had pondered this fact for a long time, but she didn't feel he and his wife were right for each other. Besides, if it ever came down to sleeping with him, which she doubted very much it would, she probably wouldn't go through with it. Just the fact that he was now giving her attention was enough for right the moment.

Even though it was enough, the real question was, would it be enough for later? It didn't matter; she would never let it come to that.

She promised herself.

CHAPTER 7

I t was seven o'clock and the hot sweltering summer sun was still beating down hard on the pavement. Jordan spent most of the evening trying to emulate the makeup job Terry had previously done for her. She came close a few times, but she never got it exactly like he had. She had to learn and learn soon.

Terry had gone to visit one of his boy toys and might not be coming home. She never knew. In any case, she had to be prepared to do it herself the next morning. He already had given her outfits for the week so she was good in that department and if she tied her hair up for the evening and put a little spritz on it like Terry suggested, her hair would be okay, too. It was just this makeup thing! If she were able, she would've had Terry put it on the night before. Then all she would need to do was get up and go in the morning.

She had just begun her fifth try of putting on liquid eyeliner when the ringing phone startled her. She grabbed some toilet paper and quickly dabbed at her eye, which now had the stinging, gooey black liquid in it.

Who invented this crap anyway?

With her one good eye, she saw her way over to the phone and picked it up. She was sure it was Terry calling to tell her what she knew all along; he wasn't coming home, hence making her attempt to put this black gummy junk on her face herself.

Only when she picked up the phone and said hello did she find out that it wasn't her roommate. It was a male though. She figured Terry must've forgotten he had another date. He did that on the regular. Now she would have to come up with another excuse for his behind and fast to keep him in the good with this fool on the line.

"Hello?" The voice was a deep baritone that sounded vaguely familiar.

Why did she know this voice but she couldn't place it? Whoever it was, it sounded good.

"I'm looking for Miss Jordan Overton."

Must be a solicitor or a friggin' bill collector. She cleared her throat and then deepened it before speaking.

"Uh, she's not here right now. Could I take a message?"

Jordan wasn't dumb. She was always two steps ahead of bill collectors. At least they got her name right this time.

The voice hesitated for a moment before speaking again.

"Could you please tell her to call Mr. Trent Prescott at the office? I'm having problems printing again and I know she'd be able to help me."

She almost dropped the phone on the floor where it would've joined her jaw.

She didn't know what to say. Trent Prescott had her number and was calling her...at home.

"Hello?" His voice made her tremble.

"Uh, yeah. I'll tell her as soon as she comes in, which should be any minute now. I'm sure she'll call you right back as soon as she walks in the door."

Damn. She forgot to lower her voice. She hoped he didn't recognize it.

He didn't seem to notice.

"Thanks then." He hung up, leaving her standing and holding the open end of the receiver. The liquid eyeliner ran down onto her cheek, leaving an elongated, dark streak from her eye to the curve of her chin.

She placed the phone back onto the cradle while debating upon how long she should take to call him back. She had to wait at least fifteen minutes to make it look good. Or did she? She could call now and pretend she was just walking in the door as her…sister, yeah, as her twin sister was hanging up the phone. That could explain why they sounded so similar on the phone. Then again, if he ever asked her about "her twin sister," she would have to lie and keep up that sham forever, or for at least as long as they worked together.

She decided to wait for at least thirty minutes. That would give her time to come up with a valid excuse as to why she wasn't home and who that could've been that answered her phone.

After the longest twenty-eight minutes of her life, she picked up the phone and dialed the office and got the voice recording. She pressed Hines' extension and his phone started ringing.

"Trent Prescott," he answered.

Jordan immediately recognized his voice. Even if he didn't identify himself right away, there was no mistaking that voice now.

"Mr. Prescott, I just got the message that you called." She tried to steady her voice.

"Who is this?"

Now she felt stupid.

"I'm sorry. It's me, Jordan."

"Oh, hey, Jordan. That was quick." His tone was more casual once he realized it was her.

She was ready to break out in excuse as to where she was and who answered her phone earlier when he spoke first and she didn't have to.

"I tried that trick for printing and, of course, it didn't work for me. I have this thirty-page report that I need to get sent out today and this damn thing won't print and Charlotte left for the evening."

She wasn't sure what he was asking.

"Would it be too much trouble for you to come in and help me out? I know you don't live far from the office and we would definitely pay you overtime."

She heard his keyboard being pressed in panic over the phone.

She looked at herself in the mirror. She already had taken her makeup off, all except the eyeliner, and still had not perfected Terry's technique of makeup application.

And how did he know how far she lived?

The coming-in part was no problem. She could hop on the bus and be there in thirty minutes. She just didn't want him to see her without her made-up face. Especially after how good she had looked earlier. But how could she say no?

She bit down hard on her lip.

"Sure. That shouldn't be a problem. I can be there in about an hour?" She looked around the room in a panic, trying to figure out how she was going to swing it.

"That's great. I'll have quite a few things to print by then. I promise I won't keep you long." He hung up and left her with the open-ended receiver again.

Now what? Which boy toy did Terry say he was going to conquer?

Maybe if she could figure it out, she could call him home for her emergency and he could hook her up again. But he'd never make it in an hour. He made her sick. He was never home when she needed him the most.

Jordan quickly jumped in a lukewarm shower as to not puff-ify her hair. Then she got dressed, throwing on the same skirt and blouse she had on earlier. Terry had only given her enough outfits for the week and she needed to save them. Besides, it could look like she just came home from work and ran out the door to help him in his time of need. That wasn't the problem though. The problem was the face.

She attempted three more times before she threw down the

mascara in disgust. How did it always end up smudged under her eyes instead of on her eyelashes where it belonged?

She contemplated calling him back and telling him that she had an emergency and couldn't come in to help him out when the door opened and she heard Terry's wonderful harmonious voice.

"That motherfucka don't know what he's missing. How's he gonna try to play me with some other asshole calling him and he knew we were supposed to be seeing each other exclusively. Bitch!" He was shouting loudly, obviously not realizing she was home and that he had just described himself to the tee.

When Jordan appeared from the bathroom, he didn't skip a beat and continued on with his childish ranting.

"Girl, lemmie tell you about these triflin' men out there..."

"Terry, I'd love to hear it," she interrupted. "But I can't right now. I need your help. I have to go back to work and I need you to make up my face again."

He finally calmed down and focused on her, but in confusion.

"What's all this? Why are you all dressed?" He looked at her from head to toe.

"I told you that I have to go back to work. I was called in and I need you to make up my face again. Please." She added the "please" for the desperate effect.

"Fine. Come on and lemmie fix that mess you attempted."

He looked at her face a little closer and scrunched up his nose.

"What in the hell? You look like a member of the Insane Clown Posse on crack."

Insult away, just as long as he hooked her up.

"You look like Carrie the day after." He laughed to himself.

He directed her to the bathroom, grabbed a washcloth and started blotting off the thick, black mass under her eyes.

"Why do you have to go back to work?" He looked down at her outfit. "And why are you wearing that again?"

Jordan looked down at herself as if she hadn't the slightest idea what he was talking about. With his hand he pushed her head back up under her chin and continued to dab at the blotches on her face.

"What's wrong with this outfit? I wore this to work today and everyone loved it."

"My point exactly. You already wore it. You don't want Prescott to see you in it again. Plus, it looks wrinkled. Dang, don't you know how to iron?"

She never said that Mr. Prescott was going to be there. She just said that she had to go back to work.

"Who said he was gonna be there?" She closed her eyes a little tighter. He was getting just a bit too rough with that washcloth.

He sucked his teeth.

"Girl, do I look stupid? There is no way in hell you are going back up in that piece to do some extra work. You wouldn't do extra work for those bastards if they paid you triple time in cash, tax-free. Now tell me where you're really going?"

"What? Seriously, I have to go back to work. He called here and needs me to print something out for him?"

He stopped wiping at her face while still holding her chin between his index finger and thumb.

"You mean to tell me that he called you all the way back to work to print something for him?"

He went back to work, dabbing at her face.

"There's no one else who's already there that can print his junk out for him?"

"What about that secretary of his? Charlotte something or other."

Just then she realized exactly how much she talked about him.

Jordan slapped his hand away. "Dang, that's enough, it should be off by now. It feels like my skin is anyway."

"Hmmmmm, I still don't see how that makes any sense." He completely ignored her and led her to his room. Nothing she said was going to make him believe she was just going there to help him out.

"He's working in Hines' office and I'm the only one that knows how to print on that computer, so obviously, he needs me there." She made one last attempt anyway.

The effort was wasted on deaf ears. He just glanced sideways at her, still not believing her story.

"Yeah, okay, and I'm Johnboy about to go to bed. Goodnight, Mary Sue." He cut his eyes.

"Just don't be actin' all stupid up in there."

Her? No way. Not a chance.

CHAPTER 8

B y the time Terry had finished with her, Jordan was looking even better than she had that morning. He had given her another one of his outfits, a pretty sleeveless floral-print dress. He had even tightened up her curls, making her hair burst with body and shine. He made up her face again, but since it was evening, he put on more dramatic makeup, but not vampish. It gave her what he called his "nighttime boudoir look."

When she stepped up onto the bus, she instantly saw the old lady who rode the bus with her in the mornings. She politely acknowledged her with a simple smile and purposely sat two rows ahead of her to face straight ahead.

This woman must live on this bus.

She gazed out the window and up toward the prominent blue sky that was speckled with vivid orange and yellow highlights. The dwindling sun began to descend across the horizon, presenting the earth with a cool, dark shadow. The warmth of the sun against her skin made her feel sexy and warm inside.

She couldn't believe he had called her back to work. What if Terry was right? What if he just wanted her to come back? Could this married man with his model wife actually be interested in her?

That reminded her of seeing Hines and Mrs. Prescott together at lunch. Now that was really a peculiar sight.

Jordan was sure they knew each other very well, considering her husband worked with Hines on a daily basis, but why would they get together outside of the office? Then again, maybe they had just bumped into each other. Regardless, she made a mental note to ask Gerald about it. He had acted so strangely at lunch so she didn't bring it up then.

She looked down at her palms, and they felt slightly clammy. She had to get herself and her thoughts together before seeing Mr. Prescott. She was actually nervous. She had never really been one-on-one with him before; especially after hours. Every time she was near him, it was only for a few moments or someone else would be in the room with them.

The old lady moved from two rows behind her and now sat directly next to her, six inches from her face.

"Every time I see you, you look different."

What was she supposed to say to that? It wasn't like she was complimenting her new look. She just said she looked different.

"Yeah, I put on a little makeup tonight."

"If you have a hot date, you should've made him pick you up instead of riding this raggedy bus." She paused and pulled something out of her purse. "That's the problem with these young boys these days. They don't know how to treat a lady."

"No, no date." Jordan turned to look out the sullied window. Hopefully this lady would get the message.

The old lady blew her nose with a frayed piece of a tissue she had pulled from her purse.

"Oh."

Another blow, only this time with gurgling mucus attached.

"It looks as though you've lost some weight, too. I'd been trying to lose weight myself, but when you get my age, you realize that you just have to be satisfied with the way you are 'cause their ain't no changin' it."

Jordan looked around the bus and saw it was virtually empty. There was a woman trying to hide a tiny dog in her purse two seats up and a young girl four rows behind them in ratty old jeans and T-shirt, clutching on to a large duffle bag for dear life. She couldn't have been any more than fifteen years of age. Jordan guessed her a runaway.

Why did this woman have to sit directly next to her and tie up her thoughts with her frivolous prattle? Not to mention her nasty nose blowing.

And where was her stop?

"What diet are you on? Maybe I should try it, even though I don't think it would do no good." The old lady stuck her chest out and rubbed her lower back. It was just like she had seen her grandmother do when she was a girl.

"No diet. I just started eating a little less and some of the weight came off."

"No exercise either?" she asked astonishingly.

"Nope."

The woman turned from Jordan and leaned over into the empty seat in front of her as if to make sure someone wasn't sitting there. When she sat back into her seat, she turned to stare at Jordan, sizing her up from head to toe. She didn't say a word, just stared.

Finally she broke her uncomfortable silence.

"They say when someone loses weight subconsciously—that means without trying," she said, now giving her a vocabulary lesson. "They're up to no good."

She paused for another moment.

"That's just what they say," she added quickly.

She arched her brows and threw her hands up in the air.

"It's just what they say," she repeated. "There's something they know they shouldn't be doing or thinking, so therefore the body reacts. Some people gain, some people lose. You got lucky."

This woman was just getting too personal now. Jordan wished the bus would hurry the hell up.

"You know, when I was about your age, I lost about thirty pounds when I was doing the horizontal tiki-tiki with a married man." She waved a small bony finger in Jordan's face.

"Well, that's not me. I'm not having an affair with a married man, or any man for that matter." Jordan spoke the words with certain valor. The truth was, the choice wasn't hers. If it were, she might have done differently. That's what perturbed her the most.

She turned back to the window and tried to enjoy her sunset. This time she prayed the old woman would get the message that their conversation was over.

"It's not just the actions that affect your body; it's the innermost thoughts. Even thoughts that you might not be aware of yourself." She bit into her apple. "Or maybe you are aware." She shrugged again. "Who knows?"

Jordan said nothing and continued to stare out the window. If she focused on something, she could probably tune this nosy woman out. Who did she think she was anyway, Miss Cleo, and she was able to read her mind? Or did Miss Cleo tell the future? Whatever. She wasn't about to give her any more ammunition.

They were now riding through the high-sidity area. She looked across the street to the park and saw a bevy of beauties walking around in next-to-nothing clothing. All of them looked spectacular. That's one thing she hated about this area; everyone was perfect on the outside and screwed up on the inside.

"You know that's what they say. . ." the old lady continued, obviously ignoring Jordan's not-so-subtle vexation with her ranting.

Jordan tuned her out again and continued to stare out the window. She nodded occasionally, as if she were still listening to her. She was really pissing her off now.

Jordan spied a long-legged brunette rollerblading in nothing but a bikini top and a pair of short shorts. She had to admit she looked beautiful and poised while skating. She could almost guarantee that she saw a psychiatrist at least twice a week and the plastic surgeon for her botox injections at least once a week. This area was a psychiatrist's and plastic surgeon's land of plenty. Oh, who was she kidding? If she had the money, she'd do the same, but thank goodness that was a choice she didn't have to make. Being broke had its advantages.

When the bus reached her stop, Jordan jumped up and walked off quickly with the old woman still talking after her. Now she'd have to occupy herself with the runaway or the lady with the hidden dog. Maybe the dog would listen but that was Fido's problem. Jordan had other things to think about.

CHAPTER 9

When Jordan finally reached the offices, she walked in toward the elevators and pressed the up arrow. She waited and waited and waited. The elevator seemed to be taking so long. If it didn't come soon, she was sure to bust from unbridled excitement.

When she thought she couldn't take it any longer, the doors finally opened and in she walked. Jordan checked out her appearance in the reflection of the doors and freely fluffed up her hair and ran her fingers down the front of her dress as she always did to smooth it out. When the doors opened again, she stepped out and walked toward her boss' office. The office looked so different after hours.

She reached the door to Hines' office and tapped softly. No one answered. She tried turning the doorknob but it was locked.

He was going to be there, right?

She tried to think back to the conversation they'd had on the phone.

He didn't just leave the information to be printed, did he?

She looked down at her desk and there was nothing. What was she supposed to do now?

Jordan decided to check Mr. Prescott's office two floors up. Maybe he was in there. When she arrived, the door was shut, but she heard voices on the other side. *He must be in there*, she thought.

Again, she knocked gently, but no one on the other side said anything. She tried the doorknob and this time it was unlocked so she slightly pushed the door open and saw Mr. Hines sitting at Mr. Prescott's desk with Mrs. Prescott and Gerald sitting on the other side. They were listening intently to whatever it was that Hines was saying. Jordan decided not to disturb them. Whatever was being said must've been something quite serious and confidential because it was in a low whisper-like voice. Quietly, she shut the door and proceeded back down to Hines' office; confused. When she got there this time, the door was open and Mr. Prescott was standing at the desk fidgeting with cluttered papers.

Jordan peeked her head in, and he looked up and waved her inside.

"Hey, I've been waiting for you." He winked as he had done earlier in the day.

"I was here a minute ago but the door was locked and no one was in the office."

"Oh, sorry. I was in the copy room and I didn't want to leave the door open. There are a lot of confidential documents in here, and we wouldn't want to give away any big secrets about our company, now would we?" He laughed.

He watched her stand in the door for a moment and then waved her in a second time.

"You can come in, you know. I'm not going to bite."

Keep all thoughts pure.

She walked across the room and met him at Hines' desk.

"So what is it that you need printed?" She walked around to see what was on the monitor.

He clapped his hands and smiled. "Right to business. I like that." He took a seat and pulled up some documents on the screen. "I need these three files printed and I need thirty copies of each."

"That doesn't sound too bad. I think I can help you with that." She smiled back at him.

This was turning out to be easier than she thought.

"The catch is, each file is approximately one hundred pages long so it may take us a little while. Will that be a problem?"

"No, I have time. I wasn't really going to be busy tonight anyway."

He grabbed her hand, completely surprising her, and kissed it.

"You are truly a Godsend. I owe you big time." He started walking toward the entrance of the office. "I'll be right back. I have to go back to the copy room. Just start printing and I'll tell you what we need to do with them after that."

"I can print from my computer, too, so we can get the files sooner and then start making the copies," she offered.

"Great thinking. I'll be right back." He disappeared out the door.

Jordan followed him out the door and walked to her desk situated right outside Hines' office. She turned on her computer and sat down, waiting for it to boot up. As she sat there, her thoughts wondered back to the hush, hush meeting upstairs, and why would Gerald be involved?

Maybe he was being fired again.

She wouldn't have been surprised, but from the looks of it, she somehow doubted that theory. And why would Mrs. Prescott be here?

When her computer finished booting up, she went to the copy room to look for Mr. Prescott but he wasn't there. Papers that had fallen from the printer were scattered every which way. She bent down and started to scoop them up when she was startled by Mr. Prescott. He had come into the room and stood directly in front of her.

She stood up and met his gaze. He reached out and grabbed the jumble of papers engulfed in her arms.

"Don't worry about these. I'll take them."

Once the papers were transferred from her arms to his, they both just stood there looking at each other. He had to have heard her heartbeat. It was beating as fast as a chef's knife against a cutting board chopping up vegetables for his specialty stew. She was scared and excited at the same time. She just *knew* he was going to kiss her right then and there. They were so close. She could even smell the mint on his breath.

"Did you get the other files to print?" he asked.

She was so breathless by now. She didn't think she was going to be able to get the words out but somehow she managed to speak.

"Uh, that's why I was looking for you. You'll need to send them to me and then I can start printing."

She never even blinked.

He stared at her for another moment and then chuckled without saying a word. He turned around and walked out of the copy room, leaving her standing there still breathless.

What was that about? She really thought he was going to kiss her but instead he had laughed at her. She had dreamt about this moment for so long and now the moment was gone, minus the kiss, one laugh added.

Jordan walked out behind him and back to the office where he was now seated behind the desk. Standing in the doorway she waited to be invited in again, but now she didn't even get that. All she got was the okay that he had sent the files to her computer and that they were ready to print.

Jordan turned around without uttering a single word and walked out of the office and back to her place, which apparently was at her secretarial desk. She was so disappointed. Then again, how was he going to kiss her with his wife in an office two floors up?

Jordan hadn't thought about it that way. They probably had come in together and would soon head out for a nice quiet dinner, leaving her to make the trillion copies.

After printing all the files, Jordan stood up and headed for the copy room to retrieve the printouts. It was almost dark and she was about ready to go home. There was no way she was going to stay by herself in this dark office building making copies. Especially while he and his wife had a nice intimate dinner at some incredibly elegant restaurant that she could only dream about.

Forget it. After this, she was out.

"Hey," he called to her as she walked past the open office door. "Are you hungry? Did you eat anything yet?"

Jordan's first thought was that this was some sort of obligatory dinner invitation, but when she looked at him, she saw anticipation in his face contemplating her response.

What about the Mrs.?

He seemed to actually want to spend time with her outside of work. And truth be known, she was hungry. She hadn't eaten since lunch and that was only a salad.

"What do you have in mind?"

He flagged her into the office again with the wave of his hand.

"I can't hear you out there. Come on in," he said.

"Hold on a minute. Let me get these papers from the copy room first. I'll be back," she responded.

He probably meant all three of them. Lord knows she didn't want to sit down and eat with *her*. The mere thought sent chills down her spine. She would tell him "no, thank you" after getting the printouts.

She walked down the dimmed corridor to the copy room and picked up a bunch of papers from the floor.

She really wished they would get this badly maintained copier fixed.

She picked up the rest of the papers and carried them to her desk where she plopped them down. When she walked past the commodious office, the lights were dimmed and the radiance of the buildings outside shone brilliantly in the huge picturesque window.

Upon walking into the office, she saw Mr. Prescott sitting in his favorite position. His back was toward her and he was looking out the window with his hands locked in a prayer-like manner. He was a king sitting on his throne, mulling over how to go about ruling the people below.

"You know, you think life is so beautiful and you think you couldn't ask for anything more, but life always throws you that curve ball when you least expect it," he said without even acknowledging her presence.

Did he even know she was there?

"Is everything okay?" She didn't want to disturb him in his serene moment, but she felt like she had to say something.

She moved closer and stood directly on the opposite side of the desk.

He swiveled around in his chair to face her.

"Everything is great." There was a look of austerity on his face. A contrast to how he was moments earlier. His voice said one thing while his face depicted something completely different.

He placed his hands on the stack of jumbled papers on the desk.

Hines would no doubt have her clean that up the next day.

"Here's the last file we need printed." He got up from his throne and offered the seat to her.

She took her now rightful place and printed the last file with him standing directly behind her. When she stood up from the colossal chair, he completely surprised her by grabbing her waist and pulling her toward him.

He looked at her with concern. He may have been contemplating whether or not to kiss her.

Contemplation done. He slowly lowered his lips to hers and pecked them softly. It was a quick but delectable kiss. He pulled back, still holding her waist and looked at her for some hint of a reaction. She could only imagine she had nothing but surprise on her face. She had expected a kiss in the copy room but this totally caught her off guard.

He leaned into her and kissed her again, only this time it was longer and there was a passion behind it. He parted her lips with his tongue and with a slight tickling sensation began to softly caress her tongue with his own. She kissed him but just as ardently. Her body trembled at the touch of his rugged hand on the small of her back, pulling her closer to him, making their bodies melt together like a ripe strawberry dipped in chocolate fondue. She felt a stir further south in her undergarments as they slowly accumulated the moisture indicating her desire for more. This was the most incredible kiss she had ever had, although, for her, there really was no comparison.

In complete surprise, she pulled back from him. Again they stood face-to-face with each not speaking a word.

Standing there speechless for what felt like several minutes, but she knew to be only seconds, she was terrified. She had no thought of where this was going next.

"Well, I had no idea someone else was in the office," a male voiced boomed from behind them.

Startled, they both turned to the door and there stood Hines.

Right behind him was Mrs. Prescott looking over Hines' shoulder, reaching for the light switch to un-dim the room.

Jordan quickly scurried from behind the desk. Of course it made the situation look all the more suspect, but how else to react to this surprise? And a surprise it seemed to be for everyone.

CHAPTER 10

"Well, hello," his wife said upon seeing her husband in the room. "Sweetie, what are you doing here?"

Jordan turned to look at him. She thought he knew she was upstairs in a meeting with Hines.

"You didn't tell me where you were going, so I assumed you were here as usual. I just came by to pry you away from all this office ickiness and take you to a nice dinner."

She said the word "ickiness" while looking at Jordan.

"Yeah, and I just came in myself and ran into Jacquie downstairs," Hines added while leafing through the stack of papers on his desk as if they carried an explanation as to why they both were lying.

Hines turned to Jordan and looked at her suspiciously.

"And why are you here? I could never get you to stay two minutes late if my life depended on it," he said with an impudent chuckle.

Sometimes, she wished it had and this could've been one of those times.

"I'm just here to help out Mr. Prescott with some of the printing and copying."

"You know," Hines said, walking up to her. "I almost didn't recognize you without your glasses." He circled around her, looking her up and down. "Your hair and your clothes are even different."

Hines' remark left her without words as she just stood there, despite him circling her like a beast waiting to pounce on its fallen prey. With one quick motion to the jugular, she would be an instant carcass.

"I knew something was different about you," Mrs. Prescott chimed in. "I'm glad someone pointed it out because I wouldn't have been able to tell. I don't think the changes are that drastic." She sneered at her.

"So you wanted to go to dinner?" Mr. Prescott questioned his wife. She turned back to her husband.

"That's why I'm here."

Oh, is it now?

"Okay, let me just get a few things off the desk and we can go." Mr. Prescott walked past Jordan and out of the office, leaving her standing with the flesh-eating piranhas ready to pick away at her bit by bit.

Once he left the room, they both directed their attention toward her without saying a word. It made her feel extremely unwelcome and uncomfortable.

"I guess I'll be going too then, if I'm not needed." Jordan turned and hastily headed toward the door.

"Actually, since you're here, you could help me with a few things." Her boss walked behind his desk and leafed through another stack of papers.

Shit.

"I printed something out and checked the copy room, but I can't seem to find it." He thumbed through all the small piles on his desk.

"Did you print this from home? If you did, your home printer prints elsewhere. Only internal printers print in the copy room." Jordan watched him angrily search for the printout.

She looked over at—or rather, kept her eye on—Mrs. Prescott who was now making herself comfortable on the leather couch situated in the corner of the room.

"No. I just printed it here a few minutes ago."

"Oh. I thought you just came in. I didn't realize you already printed. Which computer did you print it from?"

Hines, now startled by his own lie, attempted to cover up the lie with what was no doubt another lie.

"Actually, I didn't just walk in. I'd been here for a few minutes and used Trent's office for a second." He didn't look at her.

Obviously he didn't realize that that lie was also invalid. First of all, why would he go straight to Mr. Prescott's office two floors up rather than come to his own office first? And second, that would now discredit Mrs. Prescott's lie of walking in with him to pick her husband up for dinner. What lie next; they didn't see Gerald at all this evening?

"I'll check the copy room and see if there is anything left in there." Jordan attempted her previously interrupted retreat. She just wanted to get the hell away from both of them.

"What am I looking for?" Jordan asked, still headed for the door but this time not turning around. They were not going to hamper her retreat again.

"Just something that's printed on Axo letterhead."

She walked out of the office but not before taking another glance at Mrs. Prescott ,who had now pulled out a compact mirror and was absorbedly studying herself in it.

When Jordan reached the copy room, Mr. Prescott was in there looking at some printouts.

"Oh, hey." He looked up upon her entrance. "I'm just trying to straighten up some of this mess."

"The copier always does that. I keep telling them we need a new one."

Jordan didn't know if he was going to say anything about what had happened moments before Hines and his wife had walked in on them. On one hand, she did want him to say something because she wanted to know what the deal was. However, she wasn't sure if she wanted to open up that can of worms. It happened and perhaps they should just leave it alone.

"Mr. Hines is looking for some sort of printout on Axo letterhead. Have you seen it in all that mess?"

She gestured to the pile of papers muddled in his hands.

"Axo? Why would he need something from Axo?" His tone turned to one of alarm.

"I don't know. That's just what he said he was looking for."

Instantaneously, he dropped the printouts he was looking through and bolted out of the copy room leaving Jordan standing there alone…again.

She bent down and picked up the papers he had left behind and started looking through them herself.

This has been one joke of an evening, she thought to herself, slightly miffed at this point.

When she finished and didn't find what Hines was looking for, she started back down the hall to his office. When she got there the door was closed but she could hear voices. There was some discussion going on in there that was bordering on a shouting match.

Okay, this whole thing, whatever it was, was all too baffling. She wanted to listen but didn't want to get caught.

What the heck was going on? The lying; the mysterious fax from their competitor Axo; and she still had no idea how Gerald was tied into all this.

Jordan walked over to her desk and started gathering up the papers she had placed on it earlier that evening. At least that's what she wanted it to look like. Actually, she was trying to listen to what was being said behind the closed doors.

The voices got quieter.

She came from behind the desk and brazenly walked up to the door. She looked down the hall to make sure no one was around and before she knew it, she found herself with her ear to the door.

"What the hell is going on here?"

It was Mr. Prescott's voice.

"She doesn't know what she's talking about. I didn't say Axo. I said Azis." It was Hines.

"Dear, you need a secretary that can hear." There was acidity in Mrs. Prescott's tone. "Maybe if she spent less time putting on that appalling makeup and more time working, she could do her job correctly."

Jordan hated that woman so much.

"What are you talking about?" It was Mr. Prescott again. "Why are you so concerned about Jordan? I'm trying to find out why Hines here is communicating with a company that's attempting to cunningly buy us out. Besides, we all know how he deals with unwanted partners, now don't we?"

There was a pregnant pause and no one said anything.

"This has nothing to do with Jordan. As a matter of fact, this really has nothing to do with you," Mr. Prescott snapped. Good for him.

This made Jordan smile. She had never heard him challenge his wife before.

"On the contrary, my sweet." Her voice was so ice-cold; it chilled Jordan's toes right through the door. "I own a percentage of this business and I'll be damned if I see it go under because of your hurt pride."

Mrs. Prescott owned a piece of this company? Jordan had no idea. This was news to her. She figured the "C" in PRC was a silent partner.

"Anyway, even if I was communicating with Axo, what would it matter to you?" Hines' voice was the same icy tone as Mr. Prescott's wife. "And as for dealings with unwanted partners, ain't that the pot calling the kettle black?"

"Whatever. Just remember, it's definitely my business if you're planning a strategic move with our competitor that doesn't involve me. This is my company, too, and I'll be damned if you're doing anything behind my back to undermine me. I'd kill you before I let you take it from me!"

This was a tone Jordan had never heard escape Mr. Prescott's lips. He was definitely angry.

It suddenly got quiet. Jordan took this opportunity to step back from the door and look down the corridor to make sure that no one was coming. The only person she saw was a cleaning lady at the other end of the hall vacuuming an empty office. She stepped toward the door again but couldn't hear anything else. She couldn't tell if the conversation had ended and they were approaching the door she was now leaning on, so she swiftly took a step back and stared at the door for a moment. She still heard nothing. When no one exited, she went back to the copy room to clean up the remaining papers on the floor. As usual, they were all over the place. She kneeled down and started picking them up one-by-one. She reached for a fax in the corner and spotted a pair of Jimmy Choo shoes standing in the entrance of the room.

"Janice. We no longer need your help here. You can leave now."

Mrs. Prescott's voice had the same chilly inflection as when speaking to her husband just moments earlier.

Jordan locked into her eyes for a moment and what she saw frightened her. Something—namely this woman standing in the doorway—told her that she'd better finish up and leave pronto.

"I'll just finish picking up these loose papers on the floor and then I'll be gone." She dared not look at her again. She knew better than to look into the eyes of Medusa twice.

Jordan reached for an internal memo near the designer shoe when all of a sudden the shoe stepped on the paper. She tugged at it, not only forbidding her from picking it up, but ripping it into two pieces. Jordan held one end and the shoe stepped on the other.

"I said you can go!"

This time Jordan looked up at her and what she saw alarmed her.

Mrs. Prescott was looking directly at her, but her eyes were narrowed and her lips were pursed into two tiny slits.

This woman wanted her to leave and wanted her to leave now. There was no doubt about that.

Jordan stood up and was now face-to-face with her. She was close enough for her strong, expensive perfume to sting her nostrils. The smell made her eyes water.

Jordan attempted to walk by her but Mrs. Prescott stepped in her way, disallowing her getaway from this obviously incensed woman.

What the hell? Jordan thought she wanted her to leave. Why now was the queen standing in her way prohibiting her from carrying out her majesty's wishes?

"Just for the record, we're leaving soon, too, and no one will be in the office to let you in if you decide to come back for whatever reason."

Why would she come back? Hell, why would she even want to at this point?

Jordan didn't think it was possible, but Mrs. Prescott narrowed her eyes even more. They resembled a boxer who had just been beaten to a bloody pulp and had to wear the eyes of shame in remembrance of his massacre.

"So make sure you have everything before you go."

She turned and walked out of the room, ergo leaving Jordan standing there with the scent of enmity she successfully had left behind.

Jordan couldn't understand it. Had this woman sensed that Jordan detested her? Is that why she was so nasty toward her? Then again, the reason she disliked her was because she was so nasty toward her.

Rather than stand there and think about it, she quickly walked back to her desk. In passing Hines' office, she peeked into the open door. The room was completely dark but she saw the silhouette of a figure against the huge picture window. She thought it could be Mr. Prescott so she peeked her head further into the darkened room.

"Well, I'll be leaving now. Is there anything else you need?"

No answer.

Jordan looked in a little further and saw no shadows this time. She reached for the light switch and flicked it up but nothing happened. The light bulb must've blown out.

Glancing around the room, she saw no one.

Oh, well. Maybe she hadn't seen anyone. It's possible she just thought she had but could've been mistaken.

What started out to be a promising night turned out to be a total disaster.

CHAPTER 11

Jordan woke up the next morning feeling mentally numb. The previous night had been so confusing, so bizarre. She had gone to the office to be with Trent and had ended up with Trent all right—with Trent, his wife and Hines. She was sure if he had kids, they would have been all up in there, too.

When she came home that night, she had hoped to find Terry home but he wasn't. She had no one to talk to. She had no one to give the breakdown of last night's circus, with Hines as the ringleader and Mrs. Prescott as the cat woman with claws of steel.

She rolled out of bed slowly and through blurred vision, saw the door to Terry's bedroom closed. Somewhere between four in the morning and now he had found his way home. She knew this because when she got up to go to the bathroom at four, the door was open and now it was shut.

She stared at the door for a moment and started to lift her closed fist to knock but decided against it. Even though she really needed someone to converse with before she went off to work and faced those people again, she didn't know if he had company in there. So she decided against it and proceeded to the bathroom, rubbing her eyes ready to begin her daily ritual.

"Hey, girl. What happened last night?"

Terry startled her when she opened the bathroom door and almost ran into him. It was like he was in there waiting to jump out at her or something.

"Oh, sorry. I didn't know you were home."

"Yeah, yeah, but how was it last night?" he asked again.

"I wish I had time to tell you." She turned around and looked at the wall clock in the kitchen. "I wanted to tell you everything last night, but you weren't home. Now I'm running late, so get out."

He stepped past her and out of the bathroom and opened the door to his room to enter.

"I know. I had to party, but I'm here now. So what happened?" He stood at the entrance of his bedroom door and picked his ear with a cotton swab. He pulled it out, looked at it and stuck it back in his ear and began the process all over again.

"Didn't you just hear me? I said I'm late for work and I have to go." She walked into the bathroom and started to shut the door but before she did, she looked into Terry's room and saw a brand-new big-screen television.

When the hell did he get that and more importantly, how? According to him, he was broke.

Terry went into his room and shut the door but not before telling her that she'd give up details when she came home later that evening.

She'd ask Terry about his new TV that night when she came home. At that moment, she was late. Actually she wasn't really late. It was only five-fifteen but she liked to be there by seven before everyone else. It was her time to get her day started before Hines walked in, with attitude and all. She especially wanted to be there that day after the previous night's humiliation.

She quickly dressed in the black, sleek, Capri-length pants Terry had bought for her. Come to think of it, Terry had been buying a lot of things. Expensive things. He had just purchased another bottle of that expensive perfume he and Mrs. Prescott shared a liking to, and he had just bought his new male "friend" a pricey watch. At least he assumed it was for his latest "friend" because he had left it out on the kitchen table one morning, and she had never seen him wearing it. It was nice, too. It was platinum and had diamonds on he face. That must've cost a pretty penny.

She showered, got dressed and made her face up as best she could. She would give Terry the day off.

She was ready to leave but not before fluffing up her hair one last time. Walking to the front door, she almost tripped over a new pair of Nikes sitting in the foyer.

"I really have to ask him about all of this. I wanna know his secret," she said to herself as she ran out the door and down the lengthy hallway.

When she reached the bus stop, she saw that same little ol' woman she saw every day sitting there reading a book.

Oh, here we go.

Maybe she wouldn't have her words of wisdom today since she seemed so engrossed in her reading.

The woman put down her book and looked up at her without speaking a word. She did that constantly and Jordan detested it.

"My, my, missy. You are just looking prettier and prettier every day," she said as she smacked her lips together.

What a shock. Jordan began to smile and say "thank you" to the old lady until she spoke again.

"They say when a woman gets more and more attractive, but in the physical sense that is, she's got the devil in her because it's the devil that makes us see all of that outer beauty."

And right before her eyes, her compliment took a complete plunge into the Florida Everglades.

Jordan turned away and strained her neck pretending to look down the road for the upcoming bus. Still, she felt the woman's eyes on her.

"What is your name, honey?"

Jordan took a deep breath and turned around to the woman. No matter what she said, she was sure it would've been a wrong answer. She could've said Rosa Parks and the old woman would've probably still come up with an insult, telling her she should've just gone ahead and sat at the back of the bus instead of causing inexhaustible divergence between the races.

Jordan pretended not to hear her and continued her neck-strain mime looking down the road for the bus.

"Whash your name, schweetie?" This time she asked with a mouthful of apple she had just pulled out of her purse.

Jordan turned to her and saw apple juice dribbling down her chin. How the heck she was biting into that apple considering she only had like three teeth in her mouth confounded her.

"My name is Jordan."

"Who?"

"Jordan," she said again, this time a little shorter.

"Jordan?" the old lady questioned.

"Jor-dan," she enunciated slowly.

"Yeah, whatever." She took another bite of her apple.

Oh, no she didn't.

"I've watched you come to this bus stop for months now and every day your look changes." She took another bite and wiped her mouth with the back of her hand.

Was she waiting for Jordan to say something? If she was, she would be waiting a long time. Especially after the woman had practically referred to her as Lucifer himself.

"My name's Hattie." She wiped her hand on the back of her worn dress, then extended it out to her.

Jordan took her wet hand and shook it quickly. No matter what you were always supposed to have respect for your elders. That's the one thing her mother had taught her.

The bus rounded the corner with a huff of smoke trailing behind
t as usual.

"It's not old age that's gonna kill me. It's this bus."

She said that almost every day.

The doors opened and Jordan quickly hopped on the bus and
eaded straight for the back. *Please don't let her follow me*, she
hought. When she turned around, she noticed Hattie hadn't even
otten on the bus. Jordan sat down and looked out the window at
Iattie who was standing in the street still chomping away. She
ooked slightly confused as she turned and took a seat on the soiled,
ime-green sidewalk bench. She reached into her bag-lady purse
nd pulled out a book, *Gone With The Wind*. She submerged her
ead in the pages and became completely engrossed.

The bus pulled off leaving Hattie behind. It started down the
treet and down the road commencing Jordan's uncertain day. She
ad no idea what she was in store for.

How would she face Mr. Prescott or even Hines for that matter?
verything was just so weird now. She almost wished for the days
hen she just had a crush on Mr. Prescott from afar. At least then,
he didn't have to feel peculiar around him. Now she was com-
letely vulnerable. There was an attraction and it wasn't just on her
art. She had felt it the previous night. There was something there
hat she wasn't sure she wanted to investigate.

Damn, why wasn't Terry home then? She could've used some
dvice, but now she was going into this with a blind eye. She hadn't
he slightest idea what to do next, or if she should do anything at all.

Jordan looked out the window at the vibrantly lit morning sky.
"his was supposed to be the best part of the day but she couldn't
njoy it through anxious eyes. The sun was just beginning to burgeon
ver the horizon making the sky a beautiful golden hue. Before
here was that inevitable chaos of the day, there was nothing but
eace and serenity and she wanted to soak it all into every ounce of

her being until she overflowed with *joie de vivre* and forget abou
any of her uncertainties. But her apprehensiveness would not allow
her to do so.

She took a deep breath inhaling the tranquility into her lungs. I
scared her to death not knowing what was going to happen. It fel
like she needed this more than she needed oxygen and she wa
right. Something just did not feel right.

Unbeknownst to her, this day would profoundly change her lif
forever.

CHAPTER 12

Jordan quickly walked to the elevators in her routine fashion and pressed the "up" button. As she waited for the doors to open to take her to her destiny, she spied herself in the reflection of the doors again. The old woman had been absolutely correct in that she looked different. On the outside, she appeared cool and confident, but on the inside she was the ideal poster child for bewilderment.

"Bing."

The doors opened to an empty elevator.

She stepped in and pressed "2." She started to laugh thinking about her lie to Terry regarding the walking up the stairs every day and twisting her ankle tale.

She couldn't believe he fell for that load of crap.

When the elevator reached the second floor, the doors opened to complete stillness. This was exactly why she loved being there first. No Gerald, no cleaning people, and best of all, no Hines.

She walked toward the direction of her desk and saw the door to Hines' office slightly ajar.

She thought she had shut it the night before.

She tried to peek into the office while walking to her desk, but the door wasn't open enough for her to see anything. She sat down and looked at the phone to see if Hines' line was lit up.

It wasn't.

Is he here or not?

She listened carefully. Maybe she would hear movement or he would shout her name as he so habitually did every morning. But there was no sound.

She opened up her desk, pulled out a pen and slammed the drawer shut as to make blatant noise. If he knew she was there, he would definitely summon her.

Still nothing.

If she went and knocked on the door to his office and he was in a meeting or just didn't want to be disturbed, she was sure to catch hell for the rest of the day. That idea was out. It was just driving her nuts not knowing if he was in there.

Oh, well, there was nothing she could do until he bellowed for her, which could be any moment.

Jordan turned on her computer and looked at her desk with all the printouts from the previous night. She picked her purse up off the floor, got up and headed for the ladies room. She tried one last time to peek into the office. It was no use. She couldn't see a thing.

She opened the door to the dark bathroom. The only light was emanating from the small window in the rear. She reached to her right and flicked on the light.

She pulled out her brush from her purse and began to slowly brush her hair while thinking about what to say to Mr. Prescott. He probably wasn't in yet, but she could almost guarantee that some time during the day he would be coming down to Hines' office for one of his daily meetings.

She took one last look into the mirror and placed the brush back into her purse.

Well, here goes nothin', she thought to herself as she walked out of the bathroom and back to her desk to wait for the next scene of this play.

CHAPTER 13

Jordan was near hysteria and sobbing uncontrollably. The lead detective put his arm around her to try to stop her from trembling but it was no use. There was nothing to stop the abysmal shaking. At this point, the detective must've known Jordan was unable to handle sitting there with the chaos going on around her. He told her he just had a few more questions and then she could go home.

"Did you happen to see or hear anything at all that you can remember?"

He already had asked her that twice and she had told him no twice. She was going to lose it if he asked her again.

She heard a loud pop of a flashbulb go off and then a streak of lightning flashed in the overcrowded office.

The detective sympathetically patted her shoulder. "I understand you're upset and this is a horrid situation for you, but if you remember anything, we need to know."

A horrid situation? That was the understatement of the year.

After coming back from the bathroom earlier that morning, she had peeked into Hines' office again and again saw nothing. About an hour later, when she didn't hear a peep from the office, she had made up an excuse—she couldn't even remember what it was—and had knocked on the door. When there was no answer, she had pushed the door open and seen Hines sitting there in his chair turned around looking out his window at the people below. Exactly as Mr. Prescott had the night before.

Or at least that's what she had thought.

She had better say something quickly or else he was going to blow up at her for walking into his office unannounced.

"Did you find the invoice you were looking for last night?" she had asked him.

He had said nothing.

She had asked him again, but this time walked up to his desk. He couldn't have been that deep in thought, but he had been known to completely ignore her on occasion. It was his manner.

"I can look for those invoices if you still need them." She stood right across from him at his desk, waiting for his response.

He still didn't move.

Something was wrong. Something was morbidly wrong.

Although Hines was faced in the other direction, she was able to see the side of his face and what she saw horrified her.

She walked around his desk to get a better look at what she already knew. The pallid face of her boss boasted bulging eyes and his mouth was wide open. His crisp, sky-blue shirt was sodden with a deep red liquid, and there was no movement coming from him.

He was dead. Her boss was sitting here in front of her *dead!*

She couldn't scream. She couldn't yell. She couldn't do anything. Her feet felt as though they were nailed to the floor with a twelve inch silver spike.

She didn't remember exactly what happened after that. The detective told her that one of the early-morning cleaning ladies heard her scream, which she didn't recall doing, and called the police.

"Detective, we took the pictures, dusted for fingerprints and now orensics is doing their thing. Are we free to go?" A young officer cratched his head and waited for the detective to answer.

Jordan slowly walked closer to the body, tiptoeing as if she was 'oing to disturb Hines from a deep sleep. This man who yesterday .ad a velvety, dark complexion was now completely ashen. She ooked at him again, this time more closely. She noticed that his ips were a deep blue shade. One of the detectives was holding his rm and was trying to forcefully bend it to his side so he would fit n the empty black body bag lying next to him. She heard a loud rack, and the arm went down.

"Miss Overton? You may go now."

The detective quickly grabbed her shoulder and steered her away rom the ungodly sight.

"Detective, what happened? Who did this to him?"

He looked directly into her eyes and said he didn't know.

He was like one of those detectives you saw on TV. He reminded er of Columbo.

"Columbo" walked her to the office door, but before she walked ut, she overheard some of the policemen.

"Yeah, it looks like this guy was poisoned somehow and there's a uge gash on his upper torso," one of them said.

Jordan felt her legs give out from under her and she fell to her nees onto the office floor. When she was able to focus, she noticed aat her right knee was on the coffee stain that blemished his floor ıst days ago.

A police officer rushed over and helped her to her feet.

"Ma'am, are you okay? Do you need a ride home?"

She looked up at him but heard nothing.

"Ma'am, are you okay?" he repeated with a concerned look.

His voice echoed through her head as though it was contained in wind tunnel. She could barely hear him or make out the words aat were coming out of his mouth.

"I'm fine. I didn't drive. I took the bus."

When she walked out of the office and down the hall, she saw some of her coworkers staring at her. Others were straining their necks to get a peek at what was going on behind the office doors.

She looked for Mr. Prescott in the crowd but didn't see his face. Just as well. She just wanted to go home.

CHAPTER 14

Jordan reached the empty elevators and pressed the "down" button. It seemed as though everyone was interested in the police brouhaha going on. That was a welcome for her. She wasn't ready for the bombardment of questions that were sure to come.

When the doors opened, she stepped in ready to collapse. She was finally getting away from this ghastly cataclysm and none too soon. The doors began to shut until a large dark hand reached in prohibiting them from completely closing. A man reached in and pried open the doors.

"Ms. Overton? My name is Detective Ross."

No more questions. She just wanted to get out of there as soon as possible.

"I know you have already been questioned but if you remember anything else, please call me. I will be taking over this case." He handed her a card and disappeared, allowing the doors to close.

She stuck it in her purse and let out a sigh of relief.

Thank goodness he didn't have any other inquiries for her. At that moment, she just wanted to go home.

***

She had no idea how she had arrived at the bus stop but when she got there, breathless, she plopped down on the bench as if she had just run a marathon.

When the bus turned the corner, she was relieved. She just wanted this nightmare out of her mind but she didn't see how. She had seen a dead man. Not just any man but her boss. A man who had just been insulting her the night before and now he was dead. She couldn't get that fact out of her head.

She stepped up onto the bus and the first person she saw was the old lady, Hattie, staring up at her.

Oh, come on, not now, not today.

She looked past her and sat in the very last seat and scrunched down like she did when she was a kid on the school bus.

When the bus started and she realized Hattie wasn't going to harass her, she felt free to let the tears roll copiously down her cheeks.

As she did as a child, she wiped her tears with the back of her hand while sniffing profusely. When she thought she had control she lost it again and the tears began running down her face like limpid streams where they dripped from her chin and onto the front of her shirt leaving an inconsequential stain.

When her stop came, she almost missed it but jumped up in time for the bus driver to slam on the brakes and give her a dirty look. She walked toward the front of the bus and saw Hattie looking at her with sympathetic eyes.

Now that was strange. It was as if she knew not to pester her. Maybe she wasn't as non compassionate as she had seemed.

She reached her front door and looked for her keys in her purse but couldn't find them. She thought she had them when she left but now they were gone. She must've left them back at the office.

She stared blankly at the large wooden door and blinked back the tears, not knowing what to do next. She surely didn't want to go back to that place to retrieve her keys.

Just then, the door opened with a colossal swing and Terry emerged.

She forgot in all the confusion that she had paged him at work. He had rushed home to be by her side.

He pulled her inside the door and gave her a gigantic bear hug.

"Girl, I know you must be tired and all, but you have to tell me exactly what happened. I could barely understand you when you called me at work."

Jordan took a deep breath. She didn't feel like rehashing the whole thing all over again. She had done so with the police several times that morning and certainly didn't want to do it again.

He had to practically pry her purse from her fingers. He placed it on the kitchen table and steered her to the recliner and sat her down.

"Do you want some tea or water or something?"

"No, I just want…"

The truth was she didn't know what she wanted. She wouldn't be able to hold anything down in her stomach and although she was tired, she knew she wouldn't be able to sleep. She probably wouldn't be able to sleep for a long time. She would probably die from exhaustion.

Die.

Dead.

There was that word again and before she knew it she was sobbing all over again, reliving that horrible nightmare with the words she spoke to her roommate.

"I don't know what happened," she began hysterically.

"I was there last night and everything was fine. Then I was told to leave and so I did and then I come in the next morning and…" she trailed off and began crying again.

Terry got up, ran to the kitchen and grabbed some tissues and started gently blotting her tearstained cheeks.

"You have no idea who would've done something like this?"

She looked at him in surprise.

"No, I don't. Am I supposed to?"

"Someone has got to know something down there. It just doesn't make sense to kill somebody like that."

He wiped her cheek again.

"What did the cops ask you?"

Jordan took another deep breath and tried to recall. Even though the detective asked her the same questions over and over again, she couldn't remember.

"I think he asked the same thing you did. What happened and he wanted to know the last time I saw him alive and what was said."

"Well, when was the last time you saw him alive?"

"I saw him last night at the office."

Now the pieces were fitting into the puzzle.

"I came home last night wanting to talk to you so badly. So much happened last night and now it seems so irrelevant."

Terry squeezed into the chair next to her and put his arm around her.

"I'm so sorry this happened to you, girl. I can only imagine how you must feel."

She was only half-listening to him because her mind was back on the dead body that lay in that office even as they spoke.

"I heard one of the officers say that it was murder. Someone had poisoned him."

Terry let out a gasp.

"Daaaamn. That is terrible."

He got up, went to the kitchen and came back with a glass of vodka and handed it to her. Then he sat next to her again.

"Terry, if you would've seen that body and the smell. That smell I will never forget. I didn't think death had a scent until today. That whole office reeked of death. As bad as he was to me, I felt sorry for him in that chair. He just looked so helpless. It was like he didn't want to die. His eyes were open in sheer horror. Like he knew his life was about to end."

Terry nodded listening intently.

"Well, what happened last night that you wanted to tell me so bad?"

Jordan thought for a moment. The whole thing with Mr. Prescott was just so unimportant. It had been a little weird with Hines and Mrs. Prescott being there though.

When she told Terry the whole story, he cocked his head to the side.

"That is a little strange."

"Not to mention they lied about why they were there. I mean it wasn't a big deal but why lie about it?"

"Did you tell the Po-Po that?"

Jordan looked at him.

"No. What purpose would that serve?"

"I'm just sayin'. The detective told you to tell him anything relevant to this case and that just might be something important. Don'cha think?"

She looked at him again and thought before she spoke.

"No way. I know you're not saying what I think you're saying?"

She paused again.

"Are you?"

He threw his hands up in the air.

"Hey, I'm just saying. The man was murdered and it could've een anybody. If I were you, I'd at least let the detective know that omething happened there last night."

He jumped out of the chair.

"Didn't you say that you were asked to leave?"

"Yeah?"

"Who asked you to leave?"

"Mrs. Prescott."

Terry gave her an inquisitive look. It was the duh-open-your-yes-and-smell-the-mocha type of gaze.

"Come to think of it, not only did she ask, but she insisted and ne was so adamant about it."

"Why was she so insistent?"

"I have no idea. I just thought she wanted me out of there because she didn't like me. Now *that* she never made a secret of."

"What did your boy Trent have to say about this whole thing?"

"I didn't see him this morning." She dabbed at her eyes with the tattered piece of tissue.

When she heard nothing from her roommate, she looked up at him. He had his hands on his hips with that uh-huh look.

Jordan knew exactly where this was going and couldn't believe he was even thinking it.

"Oh, c'mon, Terry. Now you're sitting here trying to tell me that his wife or even Mr. Prescott could've done something like this? I suppose I'm the next one you're going to accuse."

"I don't know them but I do know you, so you're in the clear." He lightly chuckled at his flavorless joke.

She couldn't believe what she was hearing. He was accusing everyone but the kitchen sink.

"All I'm saying is that a murder took place, right?

"Right." She agreed.

"Well, someone had to have committed it, so there you go."

He walked out of the room and left her sitting on the chair pondering his last statement. The truth of the matter was he was absolutely correct. A murder had taken place and someone had to have done it.

But who and was she in any danger?

CHAPTER 15

ordan awoke to darkness outside. She must've drifted off to sleep. She'd had that same usual nightmare. It was the one where she was in a white room with the lobotomized populace promenading all about her. Again, none of them seemed to notice her. She could see the distant looks on every single one of their faces. The only thing different about the dream was the pain. This time there was none flowing through her body as it had before. She was completely at peace.

Before falling asleep, the last thing she remembered was Terry making her some tea and putting her to bed. She insisted that there was no way she was going to doze off with so much on her mind. Evidently she was wrong. Not only did she manage to fall asleep but seeing as the sun went down, she must've napped for the remainder of her excruciating day.

Terry softly rapped at her door. "Honey, are you awake?"

She pulled down the covers, got out of bed and walked to the door. When she opened it, Terry was standing there with a gorgeous pink blouse.

"Ta-da. I thought you could use some cheering up and getting something new always cheers me up." He grinned at her and gave her a playful nudge on her shoulder.

"It's beautiful." She beamed as best she could for his benefit "You really didn't have to do this." She lifted the material to he face and softly rubbed it against her cheek. It was silk. She looked at the tag on the inside of the collar. It read: Donna Karan 100% silk. Holy cow.

"Terry, I can't accept this." She tried handing it back to him bu he pushed it back in her face.

"No way. I bought it for you. Besides, it's not my size."

This was the second expensive thing he had given her during the past week. She had put off this conversation for too long, but it wa now time to speak on it.

"Terry, where in the hell are you getting the funds for all of thi new stuff?"

He turned and started walking away.

"Do you want the blouse or not?" He sounded slightly offended

She really didn't mean to upset him but this was something she had to know, hurt feelings or not.

"Of course. It's beautiful."

Following him into the kitchen, she tried another approach.

"I just don't want you to spend money on me that you don't have."

"Have some pizza. I know you love you some pizza and Pepsi." He opened the refrigerator door and reached for a white box and placed it on the countertop.

"I ordered it while you were sleeping. I didn't realize you would be asleep as long as you were." He grabbed a slice out of the bo and put it onto a plate.

"Terry." She ignored his obvious attempt to change the subject "I don't want you to get in over your head."

He turned from the plate on the countertop to her.

"Who said I was in over my head? I've picked up some extra hour at the beauty salon and have some clients who are finally paying up."

Now why was he lying to her? She had found out two week

arlier that he had left the beauty shop. She had called and they had informed her that he no longer worked there. She hadn't said anything to him because she didn't want to pry. If he wanted to tell her, e would. Evidently, he didn't want to disclose where all this money was coming from, and she didn't have the strength to argue o she dropped it.

"Oh, before I forget, some detective called you twice while you ere sleeping." He put the slice of pizza into the microwave.

"Detective Ross?" It surprised her that she had remembered his ame. She could barely even remember the face of the other detective he had spoken to in detail. She just remembered thinking that he eminded her of Columbo.

"What did he want?"

"I don't know, girl. He called twice and told you to call him back s soon as possible."

"Did he leave a number?"

Now, where had she placed that card he had given her at the elevator? It could've been anywhere.

"Yeah. I left it on the table by the phone."

Jordan walked out to the living room to the phone and looked on he table. There was no number.

"Terry," she called back into the kitchen. "Where is it? I don't ee it."

He came out of the kitchen and handed her the plate with the lice of simmering pizza.

She placed it down on the table.

"I thought I left it here. Hmmm. Now where did I put that number?" He closed one eye and looked up into the air concentrating. Maybe it would fall out of the sky.

Jordan was now getting impatient. She wanted to know what Detective Ross wanted. Maybe he had some more information on he case.

"Oh, that's right. I never put it on the table. It's in the bathroom."

She didn't even want to know.

He went to the bathroom and came back with a small piece of napkin in his hand.

"Here it is." He handed it to her.

She grabbed a corner with her thumb and index finger. Looking at the napkin, she prayed she wouldn't find any type of stain on it. It was clean.

She picked up the phone and dialed the number that was illegibly scribbled on the paper serviette.

"Hello?"

"Detective Ross, please." She grasped the phone a little tighter in anticipation.

"Hold, please."

She looked over at Terry who was standing there in expectancy. He was such a good friend. She just hoped that he wasn't in any trouble.

"Hello?" the female voice said again. "Detective Ross is in the field right now. Is there a message?"

"Tell him to please call Jordan Overton. He has my number."

She hung up in disappointment. Now she would have to wait to find out what he wanted and it was driving her mad with suspense.

"Not there, huh?" Terry slumped his shoulders in discontentment.

"No. I had to leave a message."

"What do you think he wanted?" He asked the question as though she would have the foggiest idea.

"Don't get me to lyin'. I haven't the slightest."

They just looked at each other wondering what in the world it could've been that he wanted.

She walked over to the recliner and sat down, with Terry following suit.

"Before I forget to tell you, I called the temporary service and told them you would be taking a few days off."

"Thanks, Terry. What did they say?"

"They said that your detective already informed them of the circumstances and that you would need time off."

This surprised her. It was nice of him to call for her, but he didn't have to do that. Was that a routine type of thing for detectives to do? More importantly, how did he know she was with a temp service and how did he know which one it was at that? Then again, he was a detective.

"Are you going to go back to work at that place again?"

She hadn't really thought ahead that far. Was she going back there and if she was, when?

"I don't know. I can't picture myself working there anymore."

"I wouldn't if I were you. Tell that temp service to earn their money and find you another job. This time minus the dead bodies."

She knew he was trying to lighten the mood by joking with her, but right now that was in poor taste. Just then the doorbell rang.

"Chill out and relax." He got up from his chair. "I'll get it."

Terry disappeared and two minutes later he reappeared with good-looking statue of a man standing behind him. It was Detective Ross.

Terry announced him and left the room to make imaginary coffee that no one wanted and that he knew they didn't have.

Jordan started to stand as Detective Ross crossed the room toward her.

"No, don't get up on my behalf."

She sat back down in her chair. He extended his hand.

"I apologize for coming so late but I took the chance that I would catch you awake."

She returned the courtesy and grasped his hand. He had a stiff, sturdy grip.

Detective Ross was an attractive man. Standing there, it looked as though he had to have been no less than six feet four. This made his intimidating presence even more daunting.

"Please, have a seat." She motioned to the chair next to her.

"Thank you." He sat down in the chair that looked way too small for him. His knees were practically scrunched up to his chest.

He scooted down to the edge of the seat like he had somewhere else to be in another five minutes. She imagined him to be the type that was always on the go. You probably had to be if you were homicide detective.

"How are you holding up?" His eyes told her he was genuinely concerned.

"I'm okay now," she said, lying. Although she appeared calmer she was still a wreck inside and would probably be this way for some time.

"Again, I apologize for coming this late but there are just a few things I wanted to discuss with you."

He looked at her as if he really was sorry to bother her on this otherwise beautiful summer night. He wasn't just saying that because it was in the Homicide Detective Handbook, paragraph five, section two: *Always apologize profusely for showing up at any time of day or night.* He actually cared.

"It's really all right."

He paused for a moment before speaking, as if trying to find the right words or maybe the more delicate words so not to upset her again.

"An autopsy was performed on Mr. William C. Hines and we have the cause of death."

This shocked Jordan. Detective Ross must've seen it in her face because he continued.

"It usually takes a few days but I have connections with people at the morgue," he stated pompously.

"And that's a good thing?"

He politely chuckled at her joke. He had a rich, guttural laugh.

"Nah, I guess you're right. It depends how you look at it though.

Jordan looked into his eyes. They had reverted back to seriousness he knew this was not going to be anything she wanted to hear.

"Mr. Hines was given a drug called succinylcholine, which rendered im paralyzed but still alive."

When he realized she didn't have an inkling as to what he was alking about, he broke it down into layman's terms.

"It's a muscle relaxant."

He paused for a moment as if to choose his words a little more arefully for what was to come next.

"There was a laceration on his abdomen that looks to have come om a struggle."

She remained silent and let him continue.

"To make it as plain and simple as possible, his organs were ttacked by this poison and the end result was suffocation."

Jordan tried to keep her poker face on, but it was slowly giving ay to her inner feelings.

"If that's correct, does that mean he knew he was dying?" She hoked out the words.

"It could've happened so fast that maybe he had no idea what was appening." He looked into her eyes to make sure she was still andling the information okay.

When she didn't respond he sat up further in the chair.

"Are you okay, Ms. Overton?"

She nodded but the tears stinging her eyes told a different story.

Detective Ross reached into his pocket and pulled out a handker-hief and handed it to her.

She took it and wiped her eyes.

"No, really, I'm okay." She didn't look him in the eyes because she new he would see the deception. The truth was she wasn't all right.

"We found an empty bottle of red wine on the floor. This partic-lar poison is clear and odorless and virtually impossible to detect. Ve believe the wine contained this poison. Our forensics team is esting the bottle now."

Hines drank red wine on a regular basis. As a matter of fact, he had sent her out for a bottle two days earlier. She wondered if it was the same bottle.

He leaned up further in the chair.

"What happened the night before all of this occurred, Ms. Overton?"

"Jordan," she said.

"Excuse me?"

"My name is Jordan. You don't need to keep calling me Ms. Overton," she said politely.

"Okay. What exactly happened the night before, Jordan? I know you told me you were there with him, his partner Trent Prescott and his wife. But what happened? What was said?"

Jordan quickly rewound the events of the night in her mind before speaking.

"Let's see, I went back to work around eight o'clock, then I..." She was cut off.

"Why did you go back to work? Did you plan on going back or were you asked back? Why would you go back?" He waited for her answer.

"No. I was asked back. Mr. Prescott asked me back to work."

He reached into his back pocket and pulled out a small notepad. He opened it up and produced a small red pencil that was no longer than four inches and had no eraser. He began scribbling in the notebook.

"Uh-huh." He didn't look up. "Please go on."

"Well," she began trying to remember where she had left off. "He asked me back to work and so I got on a bus and..."

"Ohhhh. So he called you at home?"

"Yes."

He reached into his breast pocket and pulled out a petite, black eyeglass case. He pulled the glasses out and put them on.

"And what time did he call you?"

"He called me around seven o'clock, I think." She answered uickly and waited for him to shoot out his next question.

Originally he had asked her to tell the story, but it seemed that she vas just answering the barrage of questions he was throwing at her.

He pulled off his glasses and held them up in the air to inspect hem. He brought them down to his mouth and breathed heavily n them eventually finishing up with wiping them on the lapel of is coat.

"I'm sorry. Go on, I'm listening." He held them up and inspected hem again.

"I know. I can't stand dirty glasses either." She watched him in musement.

"I wasn't aware that you wore glasses."

He looked at her and cocked his head to the side. "I can't see you 1 glasses."

"I mostly wear contacts now. It's just easier for me."

He smiled.

Was he smiling at her or was he laughing at her?

"So you said Mr. Prescott called you here to go back to work at pproximately eight?"

"That's right."

"I suppose since he is one of the owners of the company, he ould have access to all employee phone numbers?"

She didn't know how he got her number and at the time she didn't are but sitting there with Detective Ross, it seemed to be pretty elevant.

"I would assume so. He would need our numbers in case he ever eeded to call any of us after hours."

"Actually, I lied," the detective said.

She wrinkled her brow inquisitively.

"About?"

"Mr. Prescott is not one of the owners of the company. He is now the sole owner of the company. Mr. Hines was his partner, but it's safe to say that he is no longer."

Jordan felt sick to her stomach all over again. For a brief moment the thought of Hines' death had completely escaped her mind. He had just reminded her of why he was there.

"Are you okay?" he asked for the gazillionth time.

Jordan focused in on his face again and looked through the glasses and into his eyes.

"I'm okay," she said without any real conviction sprinkled in any of the lie that just escaped her lips.

"I can see that you're upset and you may not be ready for questions right now. It's understandable, considering the circumstances."

He put his notepad and midget pencil into his coat pocket and stood up.

"I'll come back when you've had some rest."

Jordan wanted so much to tell him that she felt ready to do this but the words wouldn't come.

"Thank you." She stood up and extended her hand.

He took her hand and cupped it in both of his. "Just take it easy, I promise you this will all be resolved soon and you'll never have to think about it again."

She laughed acerbically.

"Somehow I don't think I'll ever be able to forget. Resolved or not."

He looked at her with sympathetic and understanding eyes.

"I do need to ask you that if you can think of anything, no matter how small, please call me."

He handed her another card that she happily accepted. She seemed to feel just a bit safer with him only a phone call away. This one she would be sure not to lose.

He turned and headed toward the door with Jordan following to see him out. As he opened the door she called out to him.

"Oh, detective. I forgot to thank you for calling my temp service and giving them the circumstances. Is that customary for detectives to do?"

"No problem." He completely avoided her question and walked out the door.

As she shut the door she breathed a sigh of relief. She knew he was going to catch this guy. She looked down at the card he had given her. Detective M. Ross was going to catch this guy.

CHAPTER 16

"Thank you so much for meeting me here." Trent Prescott took sip of the double vodka martini sitting in front of him.

After Detective Ross had left earlier that evening, Mr. Prescott ad called Jordan in a panic and practically begged her to meet him t Dino's coffee house.

This place obviously served a lot more than coffee.

He took a large swig from the glass in front of him. He pulled out cigarette and nervously lit up. He took a slow, deep drag and blew out of the side of his mouth like a pro.

She had no idea that he even smoked. He took another sip and ooked at her.

"Jordan, the reason I asked you here is because I need your help. an you help me?"

"Mr. Prescott, I don't know what I can do. What do you need?"

He laughed loudly, enough for the next table to look at them in nnoyance.

"You can call me Trent, you know. I feel comfortable with you on at level and I think you do with me. Don't you?"

She wasn't sure how to respond.

"I do," she finally said.

"Good." He took another puff of his cigarette.

"I know this seemed so long ago even though it was just last night, but Jordan, we kissed in my office, remember?"

Did she remember? What kind of question was that? Of course she remembered. It just wasn't at the forethought of her mind right then considering, but of course she remembered.

"Mr. Presc... I mean Trent, of course I remember."

"I'm not going to beat around the bush, Jordan. I'm attracted to you and have been for a while now." It stunned her, the way he blurted it out. It was as if he had a real urgency to tell her.

Before she could say anything in response, he kept on talking.

"I know I'm married but that's all over. It's been over for some time now. As a matter of fact, we're getting a divorce as soon as possible. This whole thing with Bill may delay it a bit but it's still going to happen."

This whole thing with Bill? Was he unaware of the fact that his partner—and she assumed friend—was not only dead but he was killed in a grisly manner?

He must've seen the stunned look on her face.

"Don't get me wrong. The whole thing with Billy is terrible but I can't bear to think about it right now. It just hurts so much." He swallowed a huge mouthful of vodka.

She looked at him sympathetically. If *she* was traumatized, she knew how he must've felt.

He looked up from his glass and gazed at her with glossy eyes. For a minute he didn't say a word and she herself was unable to speak.

"Jordan, I have to tell you something." He looked over her shoulder and then looked back over his.

Her heart began beating faster as she looked at him with anticipation about what he could possibly have to tell her with such fervor.

"I trust you so I'm telling you this, but you can't tell anyone else until I figure out what to do." His voice lowered to a whisper.

"I won't." She whispered back, leaning over the table. She was terally almost falling off the edge of her seat.

One last puff of his cigarette.

"I think Jacquie may have had something to do with Billy's murder." Jordan pulled back from him with a gasp and looked at him with ride eyes.

"How, I mean why…"

"She was supposed to be out of town but I know she's not. She upposedly left after our meeting last night but she didn't. She's till here. Right here in town."

Jordan began to relax a bit.

"That doesn't mean anything. For whatever reason, she didn't go ut of town. Maybe she changed her mind or missed her flight."

"Noooooo," he said louder than needed. The people at the next able moved.

He was getting louder and more drunk by the moment.

"Someone overheard her." His voice went down to a whisper again.

"Heard her what?" she said in a normal voice.

"Shhhhhh." He put his finger to his lips, producing small sprinkles f drunken spit. "They heard her threatening him because he was bout to take the company from under me and go to our competitor xo."

"Who?"

He didn't answer her.

"Don't you understand? Jacquie was not having any of that. If lines took the company and sold it off, that would mess up her inerary. She had big plans for this company that would have rought in millions and millions of dollars. She had it all mapped ut and Billy was going to mess that up for her. With him gone, I ow own it all."

"But I thought she was part owner of the company, too?"

Now it was his turn to look surprised.

"How in the hell do you know that?"

She forgot that was something she had overheard.

"I heard that from somewhere. I don't remember."

He looked at her with narrowed eyes, grabbed her hand from across the table and squeezed it firmly.

"Jordan, how did you hear that?" he repeated in sober urgency.

Jordan looked down at the table and took a deep breath, then looked into his eyes. Something about this man sitting across from her looked different. It wasn't just the alcohol either. Something in his face was uncharacteristic.

"I overheard you talking last night through the office door." She waited for him to respond.

He leaned back in his chair.

"You were pretty loud in there. I couldn't help but overhear some things." She took another deep breath, giving him time to react.

He said nothing and just looked at her.

What could he have been thinking?

"What did you expect?" she said, getting defensive. "You all talk as if I'm nobody. As if I'm the invisible deaf woman."

Now it was her turn to get louder with each word she spoke.

"You talk around me, not even realizing I'm in the room. Well I'm there and I hear things." She was close to tears now.

He still held her hand from across the table. His firm grasp turned into a soft cradle.

She peered up from the table and into his face but this time she saw compassion in his eyes.

"Don't worry about it." He withdrew his hand and sat up straight in his chair. "I didn't realize we did that."

He pulled out another cigarette from the green and white pack sitting on the table and put it in his mouth.

"I just get so engrossed when I'm talking about work that I notice no one else. I didn't realize."

He reached into his right pants pocket and produced a book of matches.

Once he struck the match, he lifted the tiny fire to the cigarette until it was lit. He began to puff away, producing steady clouds of smoke like a chimney on a cold, squally night.

"What else have you heard?"

She shook her head. "Nothing."

He took another apprehensive drag while looking at her from the corner of his eye.

"It was just that night. I guess all of you were pretty excited and just didn't realize how loud you were talking. I wasn't really paying any attention but some things were just a little too loud to ignore."

"Don't worry about it," he insisted again.

The table became awkwardly silent.

"So do you really believe your wife had something to do with the murder?" she finally asked.

He flagged the waiter and ordered another double vodka martini.

"I think so." He reached into his pocket and pulled out his wallet.

"I don't understand. You said you two were getting a divorce as soon as possible."

"Yeah, so?"

"Well, if that's the case, she has no control over the company. It was yours and Mr. Hines' company. She has nothing to do with it. Especially if you two get a divorce."

The waiter came back over with the drink and placed it in front of him.

"There's just so much more to explain." He leaned back in his chair again. "You don't even know the half of it. I really don't want to get into it right now."

That was fine with her because this whole conversation was giving her a headache.

"I'm going to have to tell the police what I just told you," he said.

She immediately nodded in agreement, thinking this was something that Detective Ross should know.

He began to stand up from the table and fell back down into his seat, almost missing it and landing on the floor.

"Could you take me home?" he asked.

"I would, but I came in a cab." She looked at him apologetically.

"Well, then, could you come home with me in a cab?"

While waiting for her answer, he blindly reached around for his coat on the back of the chair, completely unable to find it.

"I don't know. I can just put you in a cab, if you want?"

"What I want is for you to come home with me, to make sure get home okay."

He gulped down the last bit of alcohol and slammed the glass back down onto table.

"Look. All I want is for you to drop me off on my front doorstep. After that, I will pay for your cab ride home. I just don't feel too well and it would be good to have someone there, just in case."

Just in case? In case of what? She didn't even want to imagine. She relented anyway.

"Let's go." She helped him up and grabbed the coat on the back of the chair that somehow had eluded his grasp for the last five minutes.

When they got outside of the coffee house, there was a cab waiting at the entrance. She put him in the cab, hopped in and off they went to drop him at home.

CHAPTER 17

Jordan woke up at four o'clock in the morning. She looked out the window at the dark night and wondered what was to happen next. It was all so overwhelming for her.

Her head was throbbing from the vodka she'd had and when she looked over to the other side of the bed, she saw Trent lying there completely still, passed out.

Why did she do it? Why???

When the taxicab had dropped Trent off earlier that night, she had walked him to the front door of his building and gotten back into the cab. When she saw him fumbling through his pockets for his keys, she knew he would most likely spend at least another hour looking for them. That is, if he didn't pass out on the front stoop first.

She had gotten back out of the cab and had probably made the worst mistake of her life.

When they went upstairs to his penthouse apartment, he seemed to have been a lot more sober than he had been while at the coffee shop, in the taxi and at his front door looking for his keys. He was sober enough to have two more drinks with her and spit out some drunken story of how he feared for his life; thinking Jacquie would now come after him. He was sober enough to kiss her and touch her and then ultimately, he was sober enough to make love to her.

As Trent lay there, Jordan thought about what she was going to say when he awoke. There was absolutely no way she was going back to that job now. It was just way too complicated. Everything was a complete mess and sleeping together didn't help the situation.

She quietly gathered her dress from the foot of the oversized sleigh bed and climbed out from under the covers in complete darkness. She headed for the bathroom with her dress in hand. When she looked back, she saw the silhouette of Trent's motionless frame basking in the moonlight that emerged from the bedroom window.

A true Harlequin romance moment.

Since she had never been to his place, she couldn't find the bathroom. When she finally located it, she flicked on the light to a room that was larger than her entire apartment. She walked over to the double sinks with the 14K gold faucets and turned on the cold water. She remembered him telling Hines one day about the purchase Jacquie had made for these faucets. He hated them but looking at them now, to her, they were in exquisite taste.

She splashed the frigid water on her face and looked for a towel to dry it. When she didn't see one, she reached for the toilet paper and began blotting her face dry, leaving tiny bits stuck to her. Nearly dry, she looked at her reflection in the mirror.

Was she crazy? How could she have done something so stupid? How did she know his wife wasn't in the area and coming home at any minute?

This was not how she had pictured her first night with Trent. He had drunkenly kissed her face and her neck and told her he loved her and had wanted her for so long.

She knew that was the alcohol talking.

In between the vodka-soaked kisses that smelled of stale cigarettes he had assured her that his wife wasn't coming home. How he knew that, she didn't know. He just seemed so pitiful that she couldn't say no to him. Ultimately, she knew she was responsible for her own actions but she was so confused.

She stepped into her dress and went back to the bedroom to look or her shoes. When she approached the darkened room, she oticed the door was slightly shut. She hadn't remembered doing hat; she thought she had left the door open when she went to the athroom. She quietly pushed the door open and looked toward he bed where she saw Trent in another position but still asleep.

She got on her hands and knees and reached for her shoes under he nightstand alongside the bed. When she retrieved them and got p, Trent was sitting up and looking at her. It made her scream.

Jordan put her hand to her chest. "Ohmigod, you scared me."

"I'm sorry."

In the shaded room, the only thing she could see was his shadow nd the whites of his eyes. It gave him a baleful look.

"Jordan, I need for you to do something for me."

"What's that?" She sat on the edge of the bed, putting on her shoes.

He reached over to the nightstand and turned on the light, evealing his beautifully chiseled face.

Now *that* was the look she remembered.

She wished he had kept the light off. She knew she was not looking er best. The mirror in the bathroom had told her so. He reached cross to her face and her immediate reaction was to pull back.

"I'm sorry. I was just going to pull off this tiny piece of tissue aper you have on your face."

She couldn't have felt more ridiculous at that point. She swiped t the right side of her face.

"It's on the other side," he said, laughing.

She brushed the other side.

"You still missed it." He reached for her cheek and gently picked ff the small piece of paper. He held it up between his fingers.

"See, I told you."

He smiled at her again and her heart just melted.

"Anyway..." The smile disappeared. "I desperately need your elp." He looked down at the bed, as if to find the right words.

"What is it?" She was getting concerned.

"Just hear me out before you say anything."

She nodded.

"Have you talked to a Detective Carmichael on the Hines case?"

She shook her head.

"No. But I did speak to a Detective Ross."

"Who?"

"Another detective on the case."

"Anyway, did he ask you where you were on the night in question?"

He emphasized "night in question" in a mocking manner.

"No, we didn't get that far. I guess he plans to finish the question ing some other time. I just wasn't up for it."

"A Detective Carmichael came around here and asked me som questions. To make a long story short, he made no secret that every one in the department pretty much suspects me of murdering Hines.

"But why?"

"I have the only motive so far. I'm the one who has the most t gain with his death."

He looked despairingly across the room.

"This is why I don't want to say anything about my suspectin Jacquie."

This still confused her. He never did answer as to whether or no she had any ownership of the company. When she had asked him another time, he had completely eluded the question.

"Why wouldn't you, especially now? You can tell them that sh has a motive, too, right?" she asked confused.

"That's just it. If I point the finger at her, it will just look like I'n trying to get them off my back and they'll suspect me even more.'

"So you need my help how?" she asked with great trepidatior realizing he never had told her how he needed her help.

"Just hear me out." He moved to the edge of the bed and sat nex to her.

"The police are going to figure out that Jacquie has a motive. I have no doubt about that."

"Well, where do I come in?" she asked edgily.

"I need an alibi and that's where you come in."

"What are you saying? You want me to lie to the police about where you were?"

"More than that. I need for you to tell them that we were together."

She couldn't believe this. There was no way she was going to lie to Detective Ross about his whereabouts the night of the murder.

"You've got to be kidding. I can't do that. I could get in trouble for that."

"No, you can't. First of all, they'll never know you lied and second of all, it would help the police to stop focusing on me and find the real killer."

He was staring in her face, waiting for a response and making her feel totally uncomfortable.

"I don't get it. Where were you? Why don't you have an alibi?"

That was the million-dollar question.

Completely nude, he got up from the bed and walked across the room. He drew the curtain slightly back and peered out the window. It was as if he were expecting someone. He turned back to her and sighed heavily.

"That's just it. I was here by myself doing some work and don't have an alibi."

"Didn't you call anyone from here that can vouch for you? They can check the records and see you were here all night. I know they can. I've seen it done on TV before." She was desperate at this point.

"Don't you get it?" He raised his voice. "I DO NOT HAVE A FUCKING ALIBI." His obstreperous demeanor frightened her.

He walked back across the room and sat down next to her on the bed.

"Jordan, I didn't do it but unfortunately I can't prove that with no alibi." His voice got softer. "They will dig and dig and catch me."

He touched her cheek with the back of his hand.

"Catch you? Catch you in what? You didn't do anything."

His eyes pleaded with her.

"Just please do this for me. Nothing will happen. Like I said, it will free up the police to find out who actually killed Billy."

She didn't know what to make of this. On the one hand, she wanted to help him, but she didn't want to lie and risk getting herself in trouble. Meanwhile, if she did this, she would help Trent and then the police could go out and find the real killer. Until this case was closed and the person was caught, she didn't feel safe at all.

She made her decision. "What would I have to tell them?"

He smiled, leaned over and kissed her.

"You are truly a beautiful person."

Uneasily, she smiled back at him.

"Here's the deal." He leaned a little closer to her on the bed. "You can tell them most of the truth."

As if that was going to make her feel better about the whole thing.

"Tell them I called you back to work but we finished up at nine then went out for drinks. After the drinks, we went back to your place at eleven."

He stopped. "You said you had a roommate, right?"

"Yeah, but he wasn't home that night."

He clapped his hands.

"Good, good. We went back to your place at eleven," he continued "where I eventually left at two in the morning."

The thought of having to tell Detective Ross that he left her place—translation her bed—at two in the morning didn't sit well with her at all.

"How do you know that covers you? What if he was murdered later than that."

He shook his head.

"Nah. Carmichael let it out that the time of death was around midnight. So I'm covered." He winked with satisfaction.

It sounded as if he'd had this already mapped out. As if he knew she was going to go along with it. He had the times down to a science.

"So it's we came back to my apartment at eleven, where you eventually left at two?"

He nodded. "Right. But don't forget we went out for drinks at nine after work."

He was saying this as if it had actually happened.

"If Detective Ross doesn't ask me where I was, I'm not volunteering this information." She spoke, as if putting her foot down when she knew better. She'd do whatever she had to do to protect Trent. However, she didn't want him to know this for fear of what he might ask her to do next.

"Oh, but trust me, he will. Just remember, nine o'clock, eleven o'clock and two o'clock."

Jordan put her shoes on and got up off the bed, prepared to leave. She had nothing to say to Trent before her departure so she just began to walk out. When she reached his bedroom door she turned and looked back at him sitting on the edge of the bed in the nude. He smiled and blew a kiss at her. He had been watching her walk out the whole time, offering no quixotic departing words after their evening of magical delight.

"Jordan," he finally said. " Thanks. I really appreciate this."

"Sure."

She turned, walked out of the bedroom, down the steps and out the front door. She stood on the other side of his front door and began to cry as silently as she could.

"Thanks?" she repeated incredulously.

Was he thanking her for the sex or the lie she was about to tell in order to save what might be a guilty man?

CHAPTER 18

I t had been days since her tryst with Trent. She hadn't heard from Detective Ross either. They were both good things. When she had come home after that exceedingly perplexing evening with Trent, Terry was up waiting for her. He claimed he was worried but she knew better. He was just being nosy and wanted to know where she was. It was ironic, but she was too embarrassed to tell him she was finally with the man they had worked so hard to get for so long. She made up some lie about not being able to sleep and going to the nearby empty bus station for some peace and quiet.

She had to practice lying anyway and wanted to be good at it if Detective Ross ever asked her about that night.

So far he hadn't. So far so good.

"I don't think you should go back to work." Terry watched her comb her hair in the bathroom mirror.

"The temp service hasn't found me another job and I desperately need the money or else I won't be able to make rent."

"I've got you covered for as long as you need. You know that."

Terry was still spending money like it was going out of style. Ever since he had lied to her about still having his salon job, she had never brought it up again. Besides, it was really none of her business.

"I can work for myself and don't need you to cover me."

She stopped brushing her hair and turned to him. "But, thank you anyway."

She really did appreciate all the support he had given her.

"Okay, girl, but if you need anything, call me at work."

She saw this as another opportunity, so she took it.

"Call you where? At the shop?"

He turned and started walking away toward the kitchen, but not before lying to her again.

"No. I have the day off there. Just page me and I'll call you back."

She wondered how he could do it. It'd been weeks and he still had the audacity to lie to her face.

It wasn't her problem. She had other issues to deal with like facing that office and facing Trent. Those were priorities one and two.

She finished up, grabbed her coat, said good-bye to Terry and walked out the door to the bus stop. When she reached the stop, Hattie was there looking as if she had been waiting for her for the past few days.

"Well, I'm surprised to see you here," she said. "I thought you done upped and moved to Mars."

"No, I just had a few days off."

"If you don't mind me saying…"

She did mind her saying, but she knew she was going to say it anyway.

"You look like you need a few more days off. What happened to you?"

"Just tired." Jordan did her neck stretching mime thing looking down the road for the bus.

"Honey, whatever has been going on in your life can't be all that bad that it can't be fixed." Hattie inhaled deeply. "Take a mirror and look at yourself. Study yourself closely. Not your outer self, but your soul. Look deep within and you'll see what needs fixin'."

Jordan turned to her and, for the first time, she was curious about what she had to say. "What do you mean?"

"If you take a mirror and look at it, what do you see? Your reflection, right? Wrong. Look hard and past all of that makeup and hair and you'll see your soul. You'll see what needs fixin' and if you have any sense, you'll fix it quick before it fixes you."

The bus rounded the corner on schedule and Hattie made her customary comment regarding how the bus was gonna be the death of her one day.

Some things never changed and right then, that was a good thing.

CHAPTER 19

ordan walked to her office building and headed straight for the elevators where there were people already waiting to go to their no doubt monotonous jobs. She would have given anything to have one of those jobs. She imagined not one of them ad the reservations she had about her position but probably still omplained endlessly about how much work they had to do, how uch they weren't getting paid, no vacations, blah, blah, blah.

The elevator doors opened and everyone rushed in. She couldn't ove. She just stood and watched them scuttle into the tiny silver ox where they stood crammed together like a pack of sardines.

The full elevator shut its doors, leaving her still standing there. he looked at her malformed reflection in the closed doors and ought about what Hattie had told her about looking deep within er soul. She couldn't imagine how she was going to fix this. There ere things that were just out of her control, consequently making er feel as though *she* was out of control. To make matters worse, ings were only going to get more complicated.

She turned toward the steps and for the first time walked up to er floor. This, she felt, somehow made up for the times she had ed to Terry about taking the stairs. It was bizarre but it made her el better. It was as if somehow she had magically reversed that lie e had told her roommate so long ago.

But now she had new lies to take its place.

When she reached her floor, she walked straight to her desk. The office was full and she planned it that way. She couldn't bear being in the office alone early in the morning. It would no doubt remind her of the day she found Hines sitting frozen at his desk.

She walked past her coworkers who just looked at her, some with the look of surprise that she would actually be there and other with pity inscribed on their faces.

Like they even had a clue as how it felt to witness the atrocity she had seen. As usual, she ignored all of them and made a beeline straight to her desk.

Her desk was as she had left it days before. No one had ever bothered to touch it. Papers were all over the place and some had even fallen to the floor where they remained stained with foot prints. Evidently, no one wanted to come near his office either. The door was shut.

Thank goodness for small miracles.

She flicked on her computer and while waiting for it to boot up she began straightening up the papers that were so carelessly laying on her desk. She bent down and grabbed the ones that were on the floor. When she came back up, Gerald was standing there looking at her.

"How are you?"

"I'm fine, Gerald. How are you doing?"

"I'm good."

He didn't say anything after that. He just turned and started to walk away but stopped and came back.

"Boy, this is really weird, isn't it?"

Jordan nodded her head while still attempting to straighten up her desk.

"You missed it. Mr. Prescott called a meeting yesterday."

This grabbed her attention. "For?"

"He attempted to explain the situation to the employees. As if hat's possible," he said with a chuckle. "Four people have already uit and Susan never came back so we don't know what she's doing. Iey, maybe the killer got her." He laughed.

Okay, it was time for him to leave now.

"Did the police talk to you yet?" He did his customary routine of oming around to sit on the edge of her desk and annoy her.

"Gerald, can you not sit so close?"

He jumped off and stood in front of her on the other side of er desk.

"A detective came around and asked a few questions," she admitted.

She wondered if anyone had questioned him.

"Really? What did you tell him?"

"I don't want to be rude, but right now, I really don't feel like get-ng into it."

"Oh, I understand."

He watched her pick up some papers off the floor for a few minutes. Ie was silent, but she could feel his eyes on her.

"If you ever want to talk about anything, I'm here."

Jordan looked at him in surprise. He was the last person she ever xpected to have some compassion.

She knew better. Anything she said would be around the office in hot minute.

"Gerald. Can I ask you something?"

"Sure, what?"

"What were you doing here that night?"

He looked at her quizzically.

"What night?"

"The night Hines was killed."

"Here? Why do you say I was here?" He didn't take his eyes off her.

"Gerald," she said with an exasperated sigh. "I saw you here with Irs. Prescott and Hines up in Trent's office."

She was really tired of everyone lying to her and for whateve reason, she couldn't figure out.

"Ohhh, that?"

"Yeah, that," she repeated.

"I stayed a little late to work on a project with Hines and then Mrs Prescott came in looking for her husband and we all got to talking."

Now *that* lie discounted Hines' lie of walking in with Mrs. Prescott At this point, she didn't care. Whatever.

"I didn't see you." He came around and sat on her desk again.

"I was here doing some work myself."

"Oh."

She didn't even bother to shoo him off again. What would b the point?

Gratefully, he hopped up on his own and started walking away.

"Well, like I said, if you need to talk, I'm here."

"Thanks, Gerald."

"Anytime." He raised his hand and whistled down the hall.

"Gerald," she called before he disappeared around the corner He turned around.

"What project?"

"Huh?"

"What project did Hines have you working on for him?"

He cocked his head to the side and narrowed his eyes. Even though he was halfway down the hall, she could see the disdainfu look on his face.

"Why, Jordan? Why do you have to know everything? Please tel me." He looked off to the side and then back at her. "If you mus know, it was just some invoice project he needed done, but I gues he doesn't need it now, now does he?"

He turned and disappeared around the corner.

What the hell was all that about?

✳✳✳

All morning long, Jordan spent her time cleaning up the work hat had sat on her desk for days. Every once in a while she glanced t the closed doors that once had been occupied by her boss.

At some point that day she would have to see Trent. He had sent memo to the employees stating that there would be another leeting at four. She figured the meeting had to do with what was n everyone's minds: their jobs and if they still had one.

Jordan looked at the closed door all day long. It was near impos- ible to do any work with the door just sitting there staring at her. he got up from her desk and walked slowly toward the large oak tructure that quite possibly separated her from her sanity. She autiously turned the knob and it opened. She stopped.

What would be the point of going into this office right now?

There was no point. But this was hardly a deterrent for her. The uriosity was way too strong. She opened the door just enough for er to stick her head in but she couldn't see anything. The office was old and the curtains were drawn making it very dim inside. She :epped in a little further and reached over and turned on the light.

Inside the office was the yellow police tape that had been torn own. It was now carelessly laying on the floor with numerous shoe nprints on it. On one wall there were camouflage-like spots and reaks. What where they and where had they come from? She didn't member those being there.

"That's what we call luminol."

She turned around, startled.

Detective Ross looked up at the streaks. "With the right parapher- alia, evidence unseen by the naked eye will appear a fluorescent lue."

She turned back to the wall. "This luminol stuff is able to locate vidence that may have been wiped away, right?"

He looked at her, impressed. "Wow. I didn't know you knew so much about forensics."

"I'm an avid watcher of *Forensic Files.*"

She looked from the wall to Detective Ross. "What are you doing here?"

"I could ask you the same question."

Jordan looked down, realizing that she really had no business in the office.

"I was, uh, I was just..."

"I understand." He smiled patiently at her. "But we really shouldn't be in here."

She walked out of the office and he followed. He turned and pulled the door tight. Reaching into his pocket, he produced a key and locked it. She figured he must've gotten it from the police.

"You never did say why you're here." She took a seat at her desk.

"Actually, I came to see you." He pulled a pad and that same mini pencil out of his coat pocket.

"I went to your apartment and your roommate Terry told me that you would be here today."

He started to laugh. "That roommate of yours is a strange one."

Jordan started laughing with him. "He hit on you, didn't he?"

"I guess that's what he called himself doing."

"Don't mind him." She sat back in her chair. "He hits on everyone."

He made her feel comfortable, the way he looked and smiled at her.

"Gee, thanks, that really makes me feel special," he joked.

Detective Ross had an incredible smile with what looked like fake teeth because they were so incredibly straight and white. She highly doubted that he was the type to spend time and money getting them done, so they had to be authentic.

"Is it okay?" He sat across from her at her desk.

Jordan didn't realize that he had asked her a question while she was checking out his teeth.

"I'm sorry, is what okay?

He looked at her like she had three heads. "Maybe I need to be sking if *you're* okay?"

He smiled again. "I asked if it was okay to finish asking you some uestions now?"

"Oh, yeah. I'm sorry, I was thinking of something else."

He smirked. "I'll leave those thoughts alone."

This brought a smile to her lips. If he only knew.

His face became solemn as he looked down at his pad, prepared o take notes.

"First, I need to ask you again if you remembered anything new?"

"Detective Ross..." she began.

"Actually, it's Michael."

So that's what the "M" stands for on his card.

"Michael, I've tried to remember anything I may have forgotten, ut everything I told you was everything I remembered."

Her line rang. She looked at him for the okay to interrupt.

He shrugged.

"No problem, I'll wait."

She hit the speakerphone. She didn't want to appear too rude.

"Jordan, it's Becky upstairs." Becky was the HR person for the ompany.

"Hi, Becky, what's up?" Jordan liked her. They had been out to unch when she first started but then she was moved upstairs so hey rarely saw each other anymore.

"A Detective Carmichael just called here and got my extension y mistake. He said he is on his way over and should be here within he next twenty minutes."

She looked over at Detective Ross for some sort of explanation. Vhy would she need to talk to two detectives?"

"Thanks, Becky." She hung up the phone.

Detective Ross looked at his watch and stood up.

"I'm sorry, Jordan. I forgot to tell you that he was coming over to question you, too. Unfortunately now that he's going to be late, don't have time to wait so you'll just have to deal with him today. Don't worry, he's a nice guy."

She thought this to be quite strange.

"Do me a favor and don't mention my name to him. Technically he's the one that should be doing the interviewing. And the fact that we don't get along too well doesn't help either."

He smiled warmly at her while gathering up his things. "I just had a special interest in this case."

What did he mean by that?

"I'll be keeping in touch." He grabbed her hand and shook it. "It was nice seeing you again."

He turned and headed toward the stairway and, in an instant, he disappeared.

She was actually grateful that she didn't have to lie to his face. It may be a little easier to lie to someone she had never met.

CHAPTER 20

"Where were you on that night?"

There it was. The question she had dreaded. She didn't want to answer but she had to because finally it had been asked.

Detective Carmichael had shown up at her desk thirty minutes after Detective Ross had left.

Upon seeing his face, she recognized him as the detective she had first encountered at the office the morning of the murder, the one that reminded her of Columbo.

Now it was him she had to lie to. He had attempted to make her as comfortable as possible that dreadful day and now the lies would be upon him.

"That night? Uh, let me see."

She looked up in the air, pretending to think about exactly where she was that evening.

Drinks—nine, apartment—eleven, left—two. She repeated this in her head a trillion times.

"Well, I came back here to work and then went out for drinks at approximately nine and then went back to my apartment around eleven-ish."

He started writing something down.

He gave her a warm fatherly smile. "Don't be nervous. I'm only asking this because I have to."

Was she appearing nervous? She thought she had said that calmly but with caution.

Deep breath.

"Jordan... were you alone that night?" he said slowly, enunciating each syllable.

Just do it and get it over with.

"No."

He looked surprised and slightly disappointed.

"Who were you with?"

Do it, do it, do it. It's too late to turn back now.

"I was with Trent Prescott."

There, she had done it.

He paused for another moment and took a deep breath.

"So you're saying after you left here, you went for drinks with Mr. Prescott at nine, then went back to your apartment with Mr. Prescott at eleven. Is that correct?"

Breathe.

"Yes, it is."

"Was it light or dark when you went for those drinks?"

Nine o'clock would mean that it was dark.

"Dark." She started fidgeting in her seat.

"And what time did he leave your apartment?"

"He left at approximately two in the morning."

"Light or dark outside?" he asked again.

"Dark."

"Are... You... sure?" he asked slowly.

Was she imagining, or was this a strange way of questioning? Her confidence level began to wane.

"Yes, I'm sure."

It was now becoming easier to lie to his face. She didn't know if that was a good or bad thing.

He scribbled something down on his pad and then put it back inside his jacket pocket.

"Thank you, Ms. Overton," he said austerely.

He stood up and formally shook her hand.

"Detective Carmichael?" She was slightly bewildered. It wasn't the questions he had asked her; it was more the way he had asked.

"Is there something wrong?" He paused and then sighed. "Ms. Overton, I think you should know that I talked to Mr. Prescott."

"And?" She was still confused.

"Mr. Prescott told me that he was with you all right, but according to him, you two had drinks around seven p.m., which coincidentally would make it still light outside. You then proceeded back to your house at ten p.m. and he didn't leave until seven-thirty in the morning, which again would make it light outside."

He looked right into her eyes.

"This of course, is according to Mr. Trent Prescott," he said surly and walked away.

When Detective Carmichael rounded the corner and she could no longer see him, she sat down at her desk with her mouth wide open in complete shock.

What had just happened here? Not only had she lied to a police office in a murder case, she was just caught in that lie and it was beyond her as to how she was going to get out of this one.

She was royally screwed.

CHAPTER 21

"I need to talk to you." She was in a complete panic as she cor-
ered Trent before the meeting started.

"Sweetheart, just let me finish this meeting and then we can talk
bout whatever it is you need to talk to me about."

He started to walk away when she grabbed his arm and held it
ghtly.

"You don't understand," she said, desperately still hanging on to
im. "I need to talk to you now!"

Before he could answer, she pulled him down the hall into an
mpty office and shut the door behind them.

"What the hell are you so excited about?" He was very much
ate with her behavior.

"We discussed this and you backed out. Why did you do it?" She
rew her hands in the air with frustration.

"What in the hell are you talking about?"

She lowered her voice to a whisper. "I lied to the police and told
em what we discussed the other night."

"What are you talking about?" he said in a panic.

"We said that we would tell the police that we left here together
r drinks at nine and returned to my place at eleven where you
en left at two." Those specific numbers would remain etched in
er memory forever.

"Yeah? And?"

She couldn't believe him. Was this man for real?

"Yeah, and?" she questioned. "Why did you tell them differently?"

"Why? What did I say?"

She shook her head to make sure she had heard him correctly.

"You can't remember the times you gave him?" This was difficul[t] for her to believe. "I don't know what you said but I do know wha[t] you didn't say."

Tears formed in her eyes and hesitantly streamed down her face[,] more so from anger than anything else.

"Shit. I thought we had the times down?"

Jordan looked at him in disbelief.

"We did or at least I *thought* we did."

Trent took a deep breath. "Okay, calm down. You're getting a[ll] upset for nothing."

Trent grabbed Jordan's arm and pulled her toward him.

"I don't really remember, but my guess is that I told him different[ly] and he told you about the discrepancy."

He wiped away her tears with his fingers, then cradled her tea[r] soaked chin in his hands.

He cupped her face in his hands. "Am I correct?"

He was taking this so lightly. It was as if they hadn't gotte[n] caught in their lie and everything was as it should be.

"Yes. You are very much correct."

"Don't worry about it. So what, there was a discrepancy? W[e] weren't looking at our watches the whole time so how would w[e] know exactly what time it was?"

She listened silently waiting for him to talk her into feeling bette[r] about the situation. He had a ways to go.

"Listen. If that's all he has to go on, then they really are up shit[']s creek in finding this murderer."

That still didn't appease her. They lied and now the police knew i[t]

"I think you should tell them what you know about your wife and ow you suspect her."

He pulled away from her and walked across the room and looked ut the window.

"We talked about that. I can't bring it up. We just have to wait ntil those idiots figure it out themselves. For all we know, they aay have gotten a clue and already know about her not being out f town that night."

He turned back around to face her.

"Besides, even if they do suspect us, we know I'm the only one ith the motive. What motive could you possibly have?" He thrust is hands up in the air. "If anybody should be worried about being aught in a lie, it should be me. Not you."

He walked over to her and hugged her.

"Oh, honey, don't worry about it. It will all take care of itself and e will be free to do as we have always been doing. Or at least nould be doing." He gave her a surreptitious wink.

He pulled away and searched her face for some sort of expression. Ie made her feel as though she was overreacting with his non-halant attitude.

He leaned in and kissed her lips with such vehemence that she lmost forgot the mess in which she had gotten caught up.

Almost.

"Come on. Get yourself together and then come out for the leeting. After that, I think you should go home and get some rest. ll call you later on tonight to see how you're doing."

He handed her the handkerchief he had in his breast pocket. He issed her one last time, then proceeded out the door but not efore she called to him.

"Trent?"

He stopped and turned.

"Yeah?"

"What happened with the story? Why did you change it without letting me know?"

He looked at her and said nothing.

"Well?" She wanted an answer.

He shrugged his shoulders. "I guess I just got the times mixed up. I'm sorry."

And with that, he turned and walked out the door, leaving her standing there to straighten up the mess before it was too late.

CHAPTER 22

It had been two days since she had heard from Detective Ross. She thought about calling him but decided against it. Besides, what would she say? Maybe Trent was right. That little discrepancy with the stories probably didn't even matter anymore. After all of this was over, she would more than likely fess up to the truth. She couldn't deal with this lie looming over her. She just hoped she and Trent wouldn't get into too much trouble.

"Girl, you have been losing so much weight." Terry stood in the bathroom door watching her get ready for work.

Terry was right. With all of this going on, she was unable to eat.

Terry had been keeping to himself so much lately. They barely even saw each other anymore. When she was coming in he was going out and vice versa. He was still spending money as though it grew on trees. This week it was a brand-new CD player and a horde of new designer clothes, some even for her. He even talked about getting a new car in the near future. Jordan knew better than to ask anymore. He had lied to her once about the beauty salon job and at this point, she told enough lies herself to last a lifetime. She didn't need to hear them from someone else, too.

"I don't feel like going to that raggedy hospital today. I should just quit." Terry had the early shift this week and was in his orderly uniform.

"You can't do that." She looked into the mirror as she brushed her hair. "Then you wouldn't have a job and we'd both be broke," she said, laughing.

"Girl, I get enough money at the shop doing them women' heads. I don't have to work anywhere else ever again."

Oh, yeah. The good ol' beauty shop. How could she have forgotten Whatever!

"You're almost a pro at this now," he said impressed as he looked at her apply her makeup. "I remember when I had to do it for you for that Mr. Wonderful Prescott."

Without saying a word, Jordan continued to brush her hair.

"Hey, you never talk about him anymore. Don't tell me your infatuation is finally over."

She swallowed hard, hard enough to be certain that he had to have heard her. The truth was, she was still "seeing" him. They had slept together the past two days and she wasn't sure what to make of it. It just seemed so ironic that she had wanted him for so long but now that she had him, so to speak, she didn't want to tell Terry anything about this affair. And that's exactly what it was... an affair.

"There's nothing really to tell." She put in her contacts.

"That's good. After all, he is married."

Married. That was a joke. From what he had told her, Jacqui had left him to live in the South of France. She had served him divorce papers, and all he had to do was sign them and he would be done with her.

Jordan was concerned at first because if she had killed Hines and fled the country, how would they catch her and prove it? Since she had not heard anything from the police, she left it up to them.

No news was good news, right?

CHAPTER 23

Jordan sat on the bus just thinking about everything that had happened to her in the past few weeks. Nothing really made sense anymore. It was like she was a completely different person. If she actually sat down and thought about it, it would probably scare her, so she opted to not think about it. *Que sera, sera.*

She also chose not to think about Detective Ross and Detective Carmichael and how they had been so nice and patient with her. And how did she repay Detective Carmichael? By lying to him dead in his face. She chose not to think about how she had slept with a married man with almost no remorse. Although he was getting a divorce, he was still married and that weighed heavily on her mind.

People made mistakes and she was by no means perfect, but still, she knew what she was doing was wrong. She just couldn't stop. Trent to her was like a drug. He intoxicated her with his juices. The way he touched her with such tenderness. He kissed her with a passion she had never known. How had she managed without him before? He talked about a future that they'd have together someday. That's what thrilled her the most. He did seem to lack some things she wasn't necessarily looking for in the past but wanted now. Things that she noticed Detective Ross possessed. He was kind and had trusting eyes. Eyes that made you feel safe.

She smiled at the thought.

"Hello, honey."

Startled, Jordan snapped out of her thoughts to see Hattie leaning over in the seat adjacent to hers.

"I don't see you much anymore. Must have a lot going on." She took a huge bite into a green apple.

"Not really."

"Then again, you could've been on the bus and I wouldn't have recognized you looking all skinny and with all that makeup on your face and hair out to here." She raised her hands to the side of her head mimicking her big hair.

"Thank you." Jordan took her comment as a compliment.

Hattie looked at her and shrugged her shoulders. "Whateva floats your boat. Personally though, I think you looked better before."

When Jordan gave her a look of surprise, she continued.

"I mean, you look good now, on the surface, but you were just the sweetest little thing before." She took another bite. "Only not so little," she added under her breath.

Jordan laughed and shook her head. If Hattie had something she wanted to say, Hattie said it. Regardless of how it came out.

"I bet you have a man," she whispered as if it were some colossal secret.

"Sort of."

She threw her hands up in the air. "Oh, man! When someone says 'sort of,' that just means they're playing hide the dragon in the dungeon."

Jordan's eyes opened wide. She never would have guessed something like that would come out of this sweet-albeit nosy-old lady's mouth.

The bus was approaching Jordan's stop so she stood up and started walking to the front.

"Sweetie," Hattie called. "Whatever you're doing can't be all th ad. As long as you can look yourself in the mirror in the mornings, ou're all right." She smiled a warm and near toothless grin.

How in the hell does she eat those apples?

Jordan turned and walked off the bus with only one thought in er mind.

Could she look herself in the mirror?

CHAPTER 24

"I'm the boss so therefore you could stay home today."

Trent reached over and pulled Jordan on top of him in the bed.

"You know I still have a lot of cleanup work to do." She planted a
.iss on the center of his beautiful, honey-sweet full lips.

She got up and sat on the edge of the bed.

"Have you heard anything else from the Mrs.?"

"Nope."

"Have you signed the papers yet?"

"Nope."

Jordan sighed in frustration. He'd been putting off the divorce
·apers for over a week. He claimed they were with the lawyer and
·e hadn't had time to look them over yet.

"Jordan, I'm gonna get the papers signed. I just have to make
·ure she isn't going to screw me over."

Jordan understood but she was getting impatient. She didn't want
·o continue sleeping with a man who was still married. They kept
·heir relationship on the down-low around the office. She knew no
·ne suspected a thing. Gerald had come sniffing around a few times,
·rying to find out any information he could get his hands on, but she
·new that there was no way he knew anything about them.

"Trent."

"Yeah, baby." He playfully pulled at her dress.

"Why is Jacquie divorcing you?"

"Why?" he repeated.

"Yeah. Why is Jacquie divorcing you? Didn't you tell me that she'd get no part of the company if she divorces you? I mean, that is the reason why you claimed she killed Hines. She wanted you to be the sole owner of the company and she had a plan for the future of the company that would make millions for you both."

Completely nude, Trent got out of the bed and walked around to her side and stood over her with his midsection directly in her face.

He reached down and put his hands on her cheeks and lifted her head.

"There's just so much you don't understand."

That seemed to be his answer for everything.

"I can't explain it to you now because my lawyer is looking into it. Jacquie's a vindictive woman. Divorced or not, she would have had her hand in the pot."

Trent sat down next to Jordan on the bed.

"Yeah, I know, but still, it would've benefited her to stay with you until after the ownership thing is dissolved and she got her piece of the business. Especially if she doesn't have any ownership in the company," she added slyly.

Jordan still had no idea as to what exactly Jacquie had to do with the company. Trent wouldn't tell her.

Trent raised his hand suddenly, making Jordan jump. He softly brought it down to her face and stroked her cheek with tenderness.

"Who knows what she's thinking, sweetheart. Don't you worry your pretty little head about it. It's all being taken care of."

Trent knelt down and started massaging Jordan's feet. While looking up at her with seducing eyes, he lifted her right foot to his lips and began gently sucking on her toes.

Jordan had no idea what "taken care of" meant and right now she didn't care.

CHAPTER 25

Nowadays when Jordan looked into the mirror, she saw someone she no longer recognized. She thought about what Hattie had told her on the bus that day. Although she had lost weight and was wearing more makeup, her face consistently looked haggard and nervous. All this time, Jordan thought she was discontent and frustrated before, but now...This just wasn't what she had signed up for. Something had to give.

Jordan made the difficult decision that she would have to have a serious tête-à-tête with Trent. Immediately. It had become a necessity for her peace of mind.

CHAPTER 26

Jordan had been at work a good three hours before Trent strolled in. When she saw him, she wanted to ask where he had been, but she couldn't because good old Gerald was sitting on the edge of her desk giving her the latest gossip.

"How 'bout that meeting? You really think our jobs are secure here?"

At this point, Jordan didn't know what to think.

"I don't know, Gerald. There's just too much going on around here and I don't even know which way is up anymore."

"Good morning." Trent leisurely ambled past the two.

Gerald stood up, practically saluting. "Good morning, sir."

Trent walked into the office and closed the door, leaving them both wondering what was going on but for different reasons. Before Gerald could even speculate as to what the haps were, Trent opened the door suddenly.

"Jordan, I'll be working in this office from now on. Call Charlotte and have her pack and move my things down here."

As suddenly as the door had opened, it closed.

Gerald waited a second before saying anything in case Trent magically appeared again.

"I wonder what that was about?"

When Jordan said nothing, Gerald pressed her.

"Do you know what that was about?"

"How would I?" Jordan was irritated at Gerald for asking and Trent for not telling.

"Jeez. You don't have to get defensive about it. I just asked question."

"I'm not getting defensive," Jordan said even more defensively "I'm just wondering why you would think I, of all people, woul know his business."

"Never mind." Gerald started walking away. "I'll let you caln down and then I'll come back later."

Lucky her.

"I'm sorry, Gerald. I've had a lot on my mind lately."

Gerald came back to Jordan's desk, obviously accepting he apology. He looked over his shoulder to make sure no one wa around and then lowered his voice to a whisper.

"Rumor has it that his wife left him and the police are looking fo her for questioning in Hines' death but they can't even find her."

So the police have finally figured out that Jacquie may have ha something to do with the murder. She and Trent were in the clea

"Where did you hear that?"

Gerald proudly stuck his chest out. "Now you know I *gits* m info. I also heard he ain't wasting no time, either. He and Charlott are rocking the boat."

Jordan wanted to ask him what exactly he meant by that, bu suddenly the door to Hines' office opened.

"Jordan, could I see you in my office?" The door slammed shu and Trent disappeared again.

Gerald gave her the uh-oh look. "Let me know what happens, he said, getting up.

Jordan nodded but had no intentions of telling him a thing. Sh knocked on the door and walked into Trent's office before he coul invite her in.

"Hey." Trent looked up from whatever he was doing.

"Yes?" Jordan walked over to what was now apparently his desk. The room had been cleaned up days before and most of the furniture was still the same. The only thing that was replaced was the black leather chair in which she had found Hines. Even the yellow tape that was so carelessly tossed all over the room days before was gone. Everything was clean.

"Has that detective been around asking you any more questions?" Jordan shook her head. "I haven't heard from him. Why, have you?"

Trent banged his fist on the desk. "Shit. That means he's still focusing on me." He raised his voice a couple of decibels.

"But I heard that they were looking for Jacquie," she told him.

Trent looked up at her in surprise. "Where did you hear that?"

"I don't know." Jordan didn't want to get Gerald in trouble for his big mouth, which had now turned into *her* big mouth.

Trent walked from around the desk and grabbed Jordan's shoulders and shook her like a rag doll.

"Where did you hear that?!" Trent shouted again.

"I don't remember. I think Gerald told me," Jordan confessed frighteningly.

Trent had this fanatical look in his eyes that Jordan had never seen before and it scared her. He softened his eyes and released her.

"I'm so sorry, Jordan. I've just been so stressed out lately. I put on this front but inside, I'm a bit worried."

"Worried about what? You didn't do anything." Now it was her turn to comfort him. "Even if they do focus on you, they'll just find out you're innocent."

Trent walked back around to his desk and sat down.

"I figured they were looking for her because you finally told them that you suspected her. Didn't you?" Jordan asked.

"I didn't tell them a thing. I told you I was waiting for them to figure it out."

"And so they must've. As soon as they find her, they'll realize she's the one they're looking for." Jordan walked around the desk behind him. She roughly massaged the taut muscles in his neck. "Relax. Everything's going to be fine."

Trent turned in the chair and faced Jordan. "I need you to do me a big favor."

"Whatever you need." If she could help in any way, she would.

Trent looked down at the ground, closed his eyes and took a deep breath.

"I need you to call the detective and tell him that it was you who overheard Jacquie talking about killing Hines," Trent said, still looking at the ground.

Jordan released Trent's shoulders and pulled away, almost falling backward. She couldn't believe what he was asking. There was no way in hell she was going to do that.

"Why would you ask me to do such a thing?"

"Just hear me out," Trent pleaded. "If they're looking for her, they must know something. Like I said, I can't say anything because it just looks like I'm trying to get the finger pointed in another direction."

He stood up and they were now face-to-face. "Jordan, if you do it, it will be more believable. They'll believe you before they believe me."

Jordan shook her head. "There's no way. We'll have to come up with something else, but not that. I could already be in trouble for lying in the first place. I'm not doing it again."

"Jordan, please," Trent begged. "It's the only way and besides what's the big deal? It will just help nail her all the quicker once they finally find her."

"Trent, if you tell them everything you heard, you can tell them exactly where she is. Didn't you say she was in France or someplace?"

Jordan was desperately trying to convince him this wasn't the right way.

"Okay, okay, okay. Let's just say that we do it your way and I'm he one to tell them everything." Trent shook his head. "If they on't find her, and believe me, she doesn't want to be found, then ll eyes on me and your detective friend will continue to search for vidence against me; even if that means making up shit. They do hat, you know. If they want to close a case, they'll pick off the first igeon they see and guess who that pigeon will be?"

Jordan walked away, shaking her head. "I won't do it."

Trent followed her and placed his hands on her shoulders while peaking delicately to her—in a whisper almost.

"I need you now. Don't let me down. You don't understand..." He ad tears in his eyes.

"I want us to be together. I want this all behind us so that we can 1ove on and be together forever."

Jordan felt her knees begin to give way for the second time. Was rent saying what she thought he was saying?

"I want you to marry me."

Jordan broke away from him and walked over to his chair behind he desk and sat down. Again, he followed. She was utterly breathless.

Facing Jordan, Trent bent down on one knee and said the words gain. "I want you to be my wife." He spoke in breathless anticipa-ion. "As soon as this divorce is done and over with, I want you to ecome Mrs. Prescott."

Jordan began to cry. Not just tears, but a cry with sobbing and all. he couldn't believe this. This was just all so overwhelming.

"Don't say anything now. Take a break. Go to lunch and get some ir and then come back and let me know."

Jordan immediately thought about Terry. How would she explain his to him? If *she* was shocked, he definitely would be stunned. He till had no idea that they were even seeing each other.

"Go on." Trent smiled at her. "Go to lunch, take a break and hink things over. I'll take you to a spectacular dinner in the city tonight to celebrate and then we'll go back to my place and mak love all night long."

"But I should..."

Trent put a tender finger to Jordan's lips. "Don't say anythin, else. Just think about us being together every night for the rest o our lives."

With his hands still on her shoulders, he stood her up, turned he around and practically kicked her out of the office. Once she wa on the other side of the door, he returned to the office and shut th door behind him where she heard a click of the lock.

Not exactly the proposal she had been waiting for all her life bu considering the circumstances.

Jordan had just walked over to her desk in a complete fog an grabbed her purse out of the drawer when her line rang.

It was Hines' private line. Trent was calling her. She picked u instantly.

"Yes?"

"I love you, sweetheart." His voice was a deep, sweet-soundin, sigh. Then he hung up without allowing her to respond.

Jordan put the receiver back onto the cradle and walked to th elevators, out the door and two blocks to a small bistro on Tent Street.

To this day, she still has no idea how she got there.

***

When Jordan returned from lunch, she went straight to the bath room to splash some cold water on her face. It was hot outside an the heat made her sweat and her makeup was running.

When she got back to her desk, the office door was still close but she could hear muffled voices. She looked at the phone on he desk and saw that Trent wasn't on the phone. Somebody must'v been in his office with him.

She sat down and huffily proceeded to finish all the work she had been putting off. She'd taken so much time off lately that it kept piling up and these nasty, cantankerous people in the office were definitely not going to touch it. Even though she had covered for them many a time.

All through lunch Jordan had thought about what Trent had asked her. Never in her wildest dreams did she ever think of being Mrs. Trent Prescott, but it was happening. All her dreams were coming true. He wanted to marry her. Maybe they would even have kids someday. They could have a boy and name him Trent Jr. or T.J. for short. She wasn't sure of any girl names. She hadn't thought ahead that far. The thought of this dream made her smile profusely. She had to tell Terry and she couldn't wait. She picked up the phone and dialed the hospital and asked for his department.

"Hello, maintenance department," said a female voice.

"Terry Horton, please."

"Just a moment," the high-pitched voice said.

While holding, Jordan could still hear the voices in the office. She stood up with the phone in hand and walked toward the door. With the phone cord stretched to capacity, she made it within a foot of the door. She leaned her head in a little further.

Snap.

The cord gave way and with a thud, she knocked her head against the door.

Rubbing her head, Jordan quickly walked backed to her desk and sat down and waited for Trent to come out and see what the commotion was about, but he didn't.

She still heard the voices; perhaps they hadn't heard a thing. She plugged the cord back into the phone and dialed Terry again.

"Hello, maintenance department."

It was the same squeaky voice.

"Terry Horton, please."

This time the woman did not put her on hold.

"Terry no longer works here."

Jordan almost dropped the phone in complete shock. "When di he quit?" She knew that they were not supposed to give out tha information regarding an employee or ex-employee in this case but to her surprise, the squeaky voice did.

"Terry didn't quit. He was fired."

"For?"

She thought she'd try anyway.

"I'm sorry. We can't give out that information."

"Thank you anyway," Jordan said and hung up.

Now wasn't that about a bitch? She didn't know how long ag Terry had been fired, but he sure enough was getting up ever morning for the past two weeks and walking out the door with hi uniform on.

This was about the umpteenth lie Jordan had caught Terry in She didn't dare think about the ones she had yet to uncover.

She thought about paging him but decided she preferred to con front him at home. This way he could tell her another lie to her face

***

About an hour later, Jordan had almost finished her invoices whe Hines' door opened and out came Gerald. He had a worrisome loo on his face and quickly scurried past her without saying a word.

Behind him, Trent came out looking as cool and collected a usual. Upon seeing her, he smiled.

"Oh, you're back. Could you do me a favor and get me som coffee?" He walked back into the office and shut the door.

That's it. Coffee? He made no mention of the fact that just hou ago, he had asked her to marry him. Jordan realized Trent wa preoccupied, but *damn*. It was like she had imagined the entir thing. Maybe she had.

The door swung open again, scaring her.

Okay, here we go now. Trent was going to pull her into the office nd really make it official with a ring and all.

Jordan began to stand up when Trent stopped her in her tracks.

"Don't get up. I just needed you to get Axo on the line for me, lease." With a loud slam, Trent disappeared behind the door again.

Jordan dialed the number with tears in her eyes. As soon as the ll went through, she transferred it to his office and immediately rabbed her purse out of the top drawer, ran to the bathroom and t in the handicapped stall and sobbed uncontrollably.

CHAPTER 27

Jordan sat on a bench in the park, watching people pass. Everyone seemed to be in their own little world and Jordan wished she could join them. She was supposed to be happy. The man she had dreamt about and fallen in love with the minute she had seen him had asked her to marry him. It just didn't seem right. How was she going to marry a man that was already married? Not to mention she didn't have any idea when he was going to get a divorce. He probably didn't either, for that matter. They would have to sit around and wait until Jacquie decided to turn up; *if* she even decided to materialize. Jordan was completely clueless as to how far the police were in this case because she was afraid to even talk to Detective Ross or Detective Carmichael. She hadn't spoken to either of them since she had lied. And from what she knew, they hadn't contacted Trent either.

Still, she wasn't sure what she was going to do about having to lie again. She had done it once so one more time shouldn't really make a difference. Detective Carmichael might not believe her anyway. For all he knew, if she did it on one occasion, she could do it again.

Across from her, Jordan watched a couple sitting on the bench. He had his arm around her and her head was lovingly on his shoulder. They looked like they were the only two people on the face of this earth, as if they were in their own little world and no one else existed. That's how Jordan wanted to feel with Trent but didn't. He wouldn't allow it. All she wanted to do was love him and she wanted him to love her even more. She wasn't totally ignorant. She knew that he wasn't in love with her right then. She figured it to be some sort of rebound issue he had about his wife. But she had no doubt that when Trent recognized what a good person she was, he'd be able to see how he really felt. No doubt.

Jordan looked at the couple again and he was now down on bended knee looking up at her. He was proposing to her and from her expression, she joyously accepted. They hugged and walked off, probably to tell their family and friends of their good news.

Now that was exactly how it should've been. Jordan languidly smiled to herself.

Someday it would be that way. All she had to do was give it some time. When Trent called her and they went out for their celebratory dinner, she would make it better. She would confess her love to him and make ardent, fulfilling love to him all night long to back up her confession. She even thought about moving in with him and finally telling everyone at the office that they were a couple. Who cared anyway? They'd find out sooner or later. Jordan could picture herself living in that glorious apartment of his. She would need a maid though. That place was just too big for her to clean by herself. It would be idyllic. They would spend every holiday together in that apartment. Christmas would be extra special. They could have a holiday party and invite their coworkers so they could all see how happy they were. She would plan a summer wedding, preferably June, and get pregnant around September or October. It would be perfect. As a matter of fact, she would tell Terry the great news. She would tell him of the engagement and of the impending nuptials. With his impeccable taste, he could even help her plan it.

Jordan jumped off the bench with a whole new outlook and ever caught a cab home. She should get used to that anyhow. No more bus for her. No more crazy Hattie. No more anything remotely close to her previous life. Things were going to be different now and she couldn't wait to begin her new venture.

***

When Jordan reached her front door, she was so excited she couldn't find her keys fast enough. She knew Terry was going to be home because that morning he had told her that he was leaving the-job-he-no-longer-had early to get ready for a big date.

When she found her keys at the bottom of her purse, she awkwardly put them in the lock and turned.

"Teeeerrrry?"

She couldn't wait to tell him the good news. Hopefully he had time to take her to some bridal stores the next weekend. He knew all the fashions of the rich and famous. She wanted him to prevent her from picking some drab looking dress with tawdry ruffles and flowers.

Jordan laughed at the thought of that.

"Teeerrrrrry?" she yelled again. "I have some great news."

When she walked down the foyer to the living room she saw Terry sitting, but he wasn't alone.

"Good afternoon," a short, older, dark-haired man said as he stood up from the chair.

She looked from Terry to the man. "Good afternoon," she managed to get out.

Terry stood up. "This is Detective Frank Carmichael from the police. The good detective came by to see you."

Jordan smiled politely. "We've met."

He looked at her from the corner of his eye.

"He dropped by your job but I guess you'd left already." Terry walked by and nudged her. She had no idea what that was about?

"I have some shopping to do, so I'll leave you two to tend to your business." Terry exited, leaving her with the detective.

Jordan would've preferred speaking with Detective Ross. Looking at the obstinate look upon his face, she would have fared much better with Ross.

Detective Carmichael stood up and extended his hand. "I apologize for not calling first, Ms. Overton, but I was out in the field and didn't come across a pay phone."

Now that was funny. He must've been the only man in this city that didn't have a cellular.

Jordan took his extended hand. He had a firm grasp and his skin was dry and hard.

"That's no problem." She put her keys down on the nearby table. "I'm not really busy anyway."

"You must've had a good day," he said.

"What do you mean by that?"

He walked a little closer to her. She could smell his strong cologne. It had a contemptible musky odor.

"I just meant that you sounded excited when you came in the door. You said you had some great news for your roommate."

Jordan walked past him and opened up a window. The smell of his fragrance was insufferable.

"Yeah, actually I did, or do."

He nodded.

The man she once saw as a father figure type had now become a sort of adversary for her.

"Would you like something to drink?" she asked.

"No, I'm fine. I only have a few minutes anyway so I'll make this quick."

"Gee, if I had to go by the look on your face, I'd say it wasn't good news." Jordan laughed nervously, attempting to lighten up the dark mood.

He looked at her with a somber look on his face but said nothing.

"What is it detective?" Now she was getting worried.

"First, I need to ask you if there is any more information that you left out."

This was her time to say something. It was now or never. Jordan thought about Trent and her impending marriage to him and the Christmas party and all the kids they would have and made her decision.

"Detective, I didn't tell you before because I wasn't sure if I should've said something, but I overheard Mrs. Prescott planning a murder."

His eyes opened wide. "When was this and how?"

Jordan had rehearsed this as she did with all her lies. Now all she had to do was deliver.

"She came into the office the other day and she and Trent were arguing about something. I didn't hear about what but when he left the room, she made a phone call that I accidentally picked up on. I heard her say that they had to do it tonight."

"Was it a male or female she was speaking with?"

"Male, I think."

She didn't expect that question.

"You think?"

"The voice was deep but I couldn't tell if it was male or female. They didn't say much. Maybe one or two words."

He took out a notepad and began writing.

She didn't know if the person was male or female? This lie was turning into a fiasco. She wanted the questioning to end before she said something to incriminate herself.

"What time was this?" he asked.

"Around eight o'clock," she said without so much as a blink.

He wrote something else down in his notepad.

"Ms. Overton, I'm going to inform you that I have been doing some checking around regarding alibis and Mr. Trent Prescott came to the office the other day with some astonishing news."

"Detective, whatever you have to say, just say it." She was getting impatient.

Why would Trent be going to his office? She thought he was trying to avoid the detective at all costs.

"He told me he wasn't with you on the night in question."

Jordan took a gasp of air, hoping Detective Carmichael didn't notice. Her heart began beating faster and faster until she thought she was going to pass out.

"He told me he made the entire thing up to protect you." He waited for her response but she wasn't able to speak just yet. "He was with friends at a late dinner and we checked it out and the story's good."

Time stood still. It was like her life had flashed before her eyes. Were they kidding, or maybe they were trying to trap her. There was no way Trent would go behind her back like this. No way. Jordan didn't know how to respond to any of this. It was as if she was in a dream, or nightmare rather.

"Ms. Overton, I need to ask you again. Where were you on the night in question?"

Why would he do that? Why would he say he lied for her when in actuality it was just the opposite? Jordan wanted to call Trent and ask him what the hell was going on. But she had to get rid of this detective first and it looked like he wasn't going to be leaving anytime soon. She had no choice but to fess up. She and Trent would have to clear him later, but she had to come clean. But was it too late?

"Detective Carmichael, I know there's no reason for you to believe me, but I was the one who lied. I was asked to make up the entire story regarding my whereabouts that night. I mean, I was here, but I was here alone."

"And who asked you to make up the story?" he asked in a sardonic tone.

"Trent Prescott." Jordan was frantic now.

He nodded but continued to look at her. Why wasn't he writing his information down?

"The only reason he asked me to lie was because he didn't want the police to focus on him." Jordan waited for a response but still he only nodded. "If they focused on him then they wouldn't find the real killer."

"And just who is that 'real' killer?" He was mocking her and didn't believe a word she said.

"Mrs. Prescott. Don't you see? She's the one you should be looking for. She's in France and she's hiding from you guys."

This time he looked at her without nodding. "You know this because you overheard her on the phone plotting his murder, right?"

Dammit. She forgot just moments ago she had told that lie.

"No. I never overheard her. I was asked to lie about that, too."

"Let me guess. By Mr. Prescott?"

"Ask Trent. He was the one who actually overheard her." Jordan found herself in a hopeless position. It was no one's fault but hers.

He cocked his head to the side. "So if he overheard her, why would he tell you to say you overheard her?"

He was really frustrating her. Everything he asked was in this galling, reproachful voice.

"He didn't think you would believe him."

He sat up in his chair. "And, we'd believe you?"

"I don't have a motive. Trent does."

He sat back in the chair and tightly clutched his hands together. "And that's the reason you intentionally lied to the police, therefore impeding an investigation."

Jordan hadn't thought of it that way.

"Well, no. I mean yes."

"I suppose you have no idea that you do have a motive?"

This completely shocked her.

"What motive could I possibly have?"

"We checked out the PHC Contract and found out that Trent owns fifty percent of the company, Mrs. Prescott owns twenty-five percent of the company and Hines owned twenty-five percent of the company."

So what? Why should that matter to her?

Detective Carmichael took a deep breath.

"Do you wanna hear the rest of our findings?"

Before Jordan could answer, he spoke up. "In the contract, Hines recently transferred his percentage to another individual."

"Why would he do that?"

"You tell me." He was being ostentatious. There was no doubt about that.

"How would I know?"

"Ms. Overton, his ownership was transferred over to you. You are now the proud owner of twenty-five percent of PHC Industries."

Jordan's pulse began to race. She wanted to pass out right there. Why would Hines have done such a thing? It didn't make sense.

"Have you ever been intimately involved with the deceased?"

Recovering from his previous statement, Jordan looked at him in a state of bemusement.

"What are you talking about?"

"I'm talking about an affair. Have you ever slept with Mr. William Hines?"

"No."

Detective Carmichael stood up out of his chair.

"Ms. Overton, I do need to advise you not to leave town. We'll be bringing you down for questioning very soon." He started to leave but turned his back to her. At this point Jordan was practically in a state of catatonia. "Oh, and incidentally, we just found Mrs. Prescott about an hour ago."

Jordan looked up at him hopefully. Why didn't he tell her this sooner? This could end the case right there, right then.

"Just to let you know, she had nothing to say regarding any of this but I guess she wouldn't; considering she's dead."

"What?" Jordan didn't think he could say anything else to shock her but somehow he had managed.

"Yep. Car accident," he said matter-of-factly.

After destroying her world with this newfound information, he offered her a piece of advice that from this day forward she probably would never be able to take.

"You have a nice day."

He turned and walked out.

CHAPTER 28

ordan spent all day calling Trent at the office but couldn't reach him. According to Charlotte, he was either out of the office or in a meeting but she tried one more time anyway. She had to speak to him as soon as possible. Before any other new developments came to light.

"I gave him your messages," Charlotte told her.

"I know, but is he in the office now. I really need to speak to him. Tell him it's very important."

"He's in a meeting. I can't disturb him. He asked that I transfer all calls into his voice mail and he'll get back to them as soon as he has a free moment," she stated in a rehearsed manner.

Jordan had to talk to him now! She wouldn't be able to wait until he had a "free moment" to return his calls.

"Tell him his fiancée is on the phone."

"Excuse me?"

"You heard me, Charlotte. Tell him his fiancée would like to speak to him right away."

"Hold on for me, please." Charlotte put Jordan on hold with the busy elevator music blaring in her ear. A few moments later she returned. "Jordan, are you home right now?" she asked.

What did it matter? Wherever she was, she needed to talk to him. This was really infuriating her.

"Yes, I'm home. Is he there or what?"

"He's here but he asked me to tell you that he's on his way to your apartment to speak to you."

Finally.

"Thank you." Jordan was relieved. This would all be straightened out soon. Now all she had to do was be patient and wait on his arrival.

When she hung up the phone she had more time to think about the events of the day. Detective Carmichael had told her not to leave town. She guessed that meant she was now a suspect. Not only was she a suspect, she just may have been the only suspect. Miraculously, somehow Trent had come up with an airtight alibi and Jacquie was dead. None of this made sense. Especially the part about her now having twenty-five percent ownership in the company that she knew nothing about. This had to be some sort of trick to flush out the real killer. In all of her lies, it hadn't crossed her mind that she would eventually become a suspect and from what it seemed, she was the number one suspect... in a murder case at that. It all seemed so surreal.

Two hours later, Jordan realized that Trent wasn't coming. She grabbed her purse and thought about leaving Terry a note as to her whereabouts but decided against it. There was just too much explaining to do and she didn't want to do it in a note. Hopefully he'd be home when she got back. Then she'd be able to sit him down and tell him everything, at last.

It was only six o'clock in the evening. Jordan figured Trent would still be there. He usually left no earlier than seven-thirty. Since she had no more money on her, she had to take the bus and just hoped he was still there when she got there.

She grabbed her keys, locked the door behind her and ran all the way to the bus stop.

When she got there, thankfully the bus was just pulling up.

She stepped up onto the bus right behind Hattie who was already at the stop. Seriously, this woman must live on the bus.

"Just made it in time, honey," she said, turning around.

Jordan ignored her and kept a watchful eye on where she was sitting. Hattie took her seat and Jordan walked five seats behind her and sat down.

When the bus finally pulled off, her heart started beating much faster. She didn't know what she was going to say to Trent when she saw him. She just hoped he had an explanation as to what the hell was going on and could make everything all right again. Nothing made sense anymore. She felt like she was going to lose it. It was like she was on this carnival ride that just kept getting faster and faster and making her sicker and sicker. She wanted to cry so badly but didn't dare. She had to keep it together and find out what she should do next. He had to have a plan. He just had to.

Hattie moved to the seat right in front of her. "You don't look so well."

"I don't feel well." Jordan hoped she'd get the hint. *If any day, today would be the day to not fuck with me. Any day but today.*

"Is there anything I can do to help?" Hattie was genuinely concerned.

Jordan shook her head as tears welled up in her eyes. There was only one person that could help and she was on her way to see him.

"I'm afraid not. I'm afraid there's nothing anyone can do at this point."

"It can't be that bad." Hattie reached into her purse for tissues.

"You have no idea." The tears began to steadily roll down Jordan's face.

Hattie handed Jordan the tissues. "I have a daughter who was just recently diagnosed with cancer."

Jordan looked up at her. "I'm sorry."

"That's something that is out of her control and only the good Lord can heal her." She looked up toward the Heavens.

Jordan managed a weak smile.

"If you don't have a terminal illness, you can fix it. Believe me on that." She handed her another tissue. "Get off your butt and fix it."

The bus stopped and Hattie stood up to get off. This was the first time she had seen Hattie get off at an official bus stop.

Well, what do you know, miracles do happen. Let's hope it can happen twice in one day.

✳✳✳

"Jordan, what the hell did you come down here for? I told you was coming."

Trent was furious at her. He actually had the audacity to be furious with *her*.

"What the hell is going on?" Jordan threw her hands in the air. "Do you know you totally screwed me?"

He walked toward her with his arms out. "Calm down."

"No! I won't." She shooed him away. One of his embraces wasn't going to make this all right.

Thank goodness all of the coworkers had left for the day because she wasn't about to hold back. The only people in the office were the cleaning people.

"You went to the police and told them I lied!" Jordan screamed.

Tears began to stream down her face again. She was mad at herself. This was exactly what she didn't want to do.

"No, I didn't!" he shouted back just as loud.

"You're telling me they lied to me? That you didn't go down there and tell them about having dinner with your friends that night?"

"Let me explain."

"Explain what? How could you possibly explain that? Do you know they are looking at me as a suspect?"

He walked behind his desk and sat down in the chair. "Just take a deep breath and calm down."

"I will not calm down!" she screamed again, this time louder. Trent's nonchalant attitude was really vexing at this point. "You asked me to lie for you and then you turn on me? I trusted you. This is my life here."

Upon hearing those words, she put her hands to her face and sobbed uncontrollably. She took a deep breath.

"What an idiot I was. Now, I'm in trouble and I don't know what to do to get out of it."

"Listen to me. I want to explain it to you."

Trent motioned for Jordan to sit down in the chair across from him. She reluctantly walked to the seat and sat down, placing her purse on the floor next to her. He went to hand her a handkerchief he had in his pocket but she declined. She wanted nothing from him. Nothing at all except an explanation.

"First of all, I only went to the police because they asked me to come in for questioning. This Detective Carmichael had it wrong. I did not voluntarily go into the station."

"I don't care if you went on your own or not. That's not the point."

"I know, I know, but when they confronted me with the discrepancies within our stories, I had to tell them the truth."

She looked at him incredulously. "Are you kidding?" she said between sobs. "But you didn't tell them the truth."

"That point is moot. I had to tell them something." He reached for the key on his desk and opened up the bottom right-hand drawer. "And so I did," he continued.

"You told them you were with friends but you weren't. You were home alone." Jordan grew silent for a moment. "Or did you lie to me?"

Trent didn't answer her.

"Why did you lie to me, if you had an alibi all the time?" Trent sighed heavily but still said nothing. "Trent?"

She was begging for a logical answer. Any answer at this point.

"I told you the truth. I was home alone. I had to lie to the police and come up with an airtight alibi." Trent chuckled. "Whoever said money can't buy everything was wrong. Money can buy anything and everything."

Jordan rubbed her temples. The more Trent talked, the more confused she became. "I'm sorry. I still don't get it."

"I needed you to go to the police and steer them off my back. There are things you don't know about me, Jordan. I'm not a completely innocent man. I didn't murder anyone but I do have things going on that need to be kept secret and if the police found out, I'd be in trouble. Big trouble."

open palms. It was as if this conversation was boring him.

"Like I said, I couldn't do it. I had to have someone else do it."

"Oh, someone like me? The pigeon? Isn't that the term you used before? The cops would need a pigeon to go after and now I've become that pigeon." Jordan was well beyond the tears. She was angry now.

"I'm sorry but when our stories fell apart and they called me on it, I had to come up with something quickly. So that's where the dinner with friends came in."

"And now I look like the murderess." She laughed at her own stupidity.

"We can fix it. You'll see. I have it all mapped out."

"It still doesn't make sense to me. If you had an alibi, you should've told them that in the beginning instead of dragging me in on it."

"Don't you get it?" Trent said heatedly. "I didn't have an alibi. When the heat got too hot, I had to create one. And so I did. I covered all my bases."

Jordan stared at Trent, wondering who the hell he was. "You mean you covered your ass, is what you did?"

Trent shook his head.

"And, at the expense of mine," Jordan continued.

The tears began to resurface again. Jordan didn't want to cry but she couldn't do anything else. She was in trouble, big trouble, and she didn't know if even Trent could fix it.

"It's cool. I promise you. By next week, it will all be taken care of."

"How, Trent? How will all this be taken care of?"

Jordan looked out the window defeated. She didn't know whether or not to believe Trent yet another time.

Fool me once, shame on you, fool me twice, shame on me.

"Do you know I now have a motive?" Jordan laughed. "Hines took it upon himself to add me to the PHC contract." She looked for a reaction from Trent but he just blankly stared at her. "Yeah, now I have a motive. So it seems you're not the only one." He still said nothing to her. He had this anomalous expression on his face. It frightened her.

"So now with Hines and Jacquie permanently out of the picture, you and I seem to be the sole owners of the company." Trent's face remained expressionless as he explained this to her.

"I guess so." Jordan threw her hands up in the air. "All of this is yours and mine, and I have no friggin' idea why."

Jordan still wasn't quite understanding what the lie was and wasn't. The way Trent so-called explained things only perplexed her all the more. Even with her annoyance with his blasé demeanor, she didn't want to press it too much with him. If he said he had a plan, he had a plan.

Trent got up from around the desk and slowly walked to her sitting in the chair.

"I'm so sorry this happened the way it did. I promise, I'm going to fix this. I love you and I want no harm to come to you. I need you right now and I know you need me. We need each other and, with each other, we will get through this."

Trent bent down on one knee and reached into his pocket and pulled out a small aqua-colored box.

Jordan's eyes opened wide in astonishment. "What are you doing?"

Trent laughed out loud. "I know this isn't the perfect moment but I can't wait any longer. I need you permanently in my life now." He opened the box and pulled out a huge sparkling diamond surrounded by platinum and placed it on her finger. "Will you marry me, Jordan?"

Now it was official.

CHAPTER 29

Jordan left the office without giving him an answer. Again, he told her to think about it and quickly dismissed her when his phone rang.

At least this time she had a ring on her finger to prove she wasn't imagining the whole thing.

She looked down at the sparkling piece of jewelry. She held her hand up in the air and let the sunlight shine upon it, making it glisten even brighter. She had never dreamt of owning something even remotely close to this.

Just the look of it made Jordan smile. It almost even made her forget about the trouble she was in; almost but not quite. They would still have to deal with the police. She figured the best way would be to go downtown to the police station together and tell them everything from the beginning to the sordid end. They had to come clean in order to eliminate themselves from the suspect list. She didn't even know if Trent was still on the list since his airtight alibi had surfaced, but she was and this was one list she didn't want to be on.

That would be another problem. They wouldn't have to say that he lied about his alibi. What's done is done. Instead, he would have to fess up to asking her to lie. If he explained why, they would have to understand that he only did it to help the police find the guilty party.

As Jordan thought about this, she realized how ridiculous it all sounded. In the end, the lies were basically told for nothing. If they would've just let the police do their job, they would have found the murderer and that would've been that. Finito.

Jordan looked down at the ring again and realized that whatever the circumstances, it would all be okay now. She was going to be Mrs. Trent Prescott and nothing was going to change that. She reached the bus stop and went to check her purse to see if she had enough money. When she went to look, she realized her purse wasn't at her side. She had left it back at Trent's office.

That's good. Now she could go back for it and get cab fare. She didn't really feel like taking the bus anyway. She had to get used to taking cabs. She thought he drove a Mercedes. Come to think of it, she didn't really know what he drove. Didn't matter. Whatever it was, it was sure to be nice. She just hoped it wasn't a stick. She tried to drive a stick once and that had been a big disaster.

When Jordan reached the elevators, she stepped in but not before seeing a woman coming down the corridor. She almost didn't recognize her but it was Charlotte, Trent's secretary. She had her long, black hair out and was in full makeup. She looked good. *Really good.* She had on a form-fitting white skirt with a navy blouse that was unbuttoned enough for anyone to get a peek at her ample cleavage. Jordan had no idea Charlotte was even built like that. She always chose to wear those drab-looking dresses. Much like the ones Jordan herself wore not so long ago.

Charlotte walked past the elevators as the doors began to close. She hadn't seen her. That was really bizarre. If she didn't just get a good look at those piercing blue eyes of hers, she wouldn't have believed it was her. Who knew?

When Jordan reached the second floor, she went straight for Hines' old office. The door was slightly ajar and Trent was inside talking on the speakerphone with his back turned, looking out of the window. Jordan's purse was sitting on the corner of his desk.

"So, is everything okay now?" a male voice said over the speaker.

Trent laughed. "You know me. I take care of everything."

Jordan was about to walk into the office until she heard the voice through the speaker talk again.

"Jordan suspects nothing then?"

Jordan took a step back and listened closer.

Trent laughed again but this time it was more insidious. "I have that woman wrapped around my little finger."

"Did she accept that ring you gave her? I still say it was too big. What a waste! And how is Charlotte taking it?"

Why did she know that voice?

"Of course she did. Come on now." Trent paused for a moment. "And Charlotte is taking it well, considering she knows absolutely nothing about it."

There was laughter from the other end.

"Hold on for a minute."

Jordan heard Trent get up from his chair and then it got extremely quiet. She thought she hadn't made a noise but maybe he had spotted her. She moved a little further back from the door to make sure she couldn't be seen. Once in place, she stood silently with her eyes wide open.

"Okay, I'm back," Trent said to the speakerphone. "Anyway, Charlotte's trying to keep it cool but Jordan's working her nerves with all this calling. You know the shit almost hit the fan when Jordan called here saying she was my fiancée."

He and the unknown guy on the speakerphone chortled hilariously at that.

"I told you, Trent. You'd better watch that. Jordan's not as stupid as you say. She's gonna come around soon and, BOO-YAA, everything will be ruined."

Jordan wondered who the voice was referring to; her or Charlotte.

"You need to take care of that soon." The guy on the speakerphone had suddenly gotten serious.

Take care of what?

"Oh, please." Trent had an air of confidence in his voice. He pivoted around in his chair and Jordan ducked. "I just gave her a beautiful—and expensive, I might add—diamond ring. She is here for the duration. Jordan's gonna be my out."

"Just don't let her find out about Charlotte because you know how women get."

"Mmmmm, Charlotte." Trent threw his head back. "Her fine ass just left here and, let's just say, I gave her an excellent go with round one."

"Now that's one piece of fine ass," the voice said.

Tears stung Jordan's eyes. She couldn't believe this. Trent had been playing her all along and he had been sleeping with Charlotte.

"Hey man, I gotta run to the copy machine. I'll get back with you." Trent quickly hung up the phone.

Jordan backed away from the door and ran around the corner in time to see him exit his office, walk past the elevators and down the corridor toward the copy room. She turned and started to leave when she realized her purse was still on his desk. She went back, ran into his office and quickly grabbed it off the desk before making a hasty retreat. As she came out of the office, she heard his voice coming around the corner. She ran in the opposite direction and hid in the corner again, waiting for Trent to go back into the office and hopefully shut the door so she could sneak out. She didn't know what would happen if she faced him now. She didn't want to take that chance.

Jordan peeked around the corner and saw Trent walk back into the office and push the door closed. She tried again to make a quick retreat but she heard the ding of the elevator. She ran to her desk and dropped to her hands and knees, crouching behind it like a little mouse running for cover. She couldn't see the face but she was able to see that it was a woman in a white skirt. Charlotte.

Charlotte stood at Hines' office door, tapping on it gently. Jordan peeked from around the desk and saw she had two Styrofoam cups in her hand.

"Hey, baby," she heard Trent call to her. "Bring that beautiful body in here."

Charlotte walked in and pushed the door up without completely shutting it. After that, all Jordan heard was kissing and moaning and then the door slammed shut.

Ding. Round two.

CHAPTER 30

"Girl, I can't believe this shit." Terry was furious.

They sat in a chair curled up together as Jordan finally enlightened Terry with the whole disgusting story from beginning to end.

"And now the police are looking at me as the murderer. They actually think I may have killed Hines."

Terry took a tissue from the box on the table next to them and dabbed away at Jordan's tears. He seemed to be doing that a lot lately. "Why didn't you tell me before? I could've told you the asshole was no good. I told you about those married men."

"Terry, I don't need a lecture. I thought I was doing the right thing. I thought he loved me."

He held her closer. "I know. I'm sorry. I'm just so pissed off that he left you in this position. I wonder if that hussy Charlotte knows about you and all this?"

Jordan shook her head. "I don't know." She was still crying in hysteria. "I loved him so much. I don't know how I'll be able to go on anymore."

Terry looked at her with disbelief. "You've got to be shittin' me. Are you more upset that you don't have him anymore or that he left you out there to take the rap for a murder?"

"I don't know. It's just that..."

"Stop it. You need to get your mind right," he said disgusted "This parasite left you out there. Ass all out and you're sorry you're not still with him?"

"You just don't understand."

Terry stood up. "You're fucking right, I don't understand. Why don't you break it down for me, please."

Jordan knew Terry or no one else could possibly understand what was going on in her mind. Hell, she couldn't even comprehend it. She really did love Trent and it hurt to lose him like this. She looked down at her ring. It didn't look the same anymore. Although it was the same ring, now it was tarnished with deceit.

Terry looked down at Jordan's finger with his eyes wide open. "What is that?" He grabbed her hand and held it closely to his face inspecting the ring. "Girl, this a princess cut platinum setting with baguette diamond accents." Jordan snatched her hand away. "He gave you this?" Jordan didn't answer. "You sold your freedom for a diamond ring?" Terry shook his head. "I hope it was worth it."

Jordan had come to Terry for comfort. She wasn't going to find that here and rightfully so. She deserved the tongue-lashing she was getting. To her, his words were like an alarm clock going off first thing in the morning, waking her up to a new day.

Terry glanced at his watch and frowned. "I've got to go in to work tonight. You take yourself to bed and we'll go to the police tomorrow and explain everything." His voice got softer. "Jordan, I know you're hurt and I'm going to do everything in my power to help you out of this situation, but you've got to do something for me?" She looked up at him. What could she possibly do for him? "I need for you to take a good look at yourself in the mirror and finally realize that you don't need to be anyone's doormat anymore."

That's how he thought of her?

He knelt down beside her in the chair. "You need to realize that you and only you can take control of your life. You made an error n judgment and now you're in trouble. But now it's time to tell the ruth and get you out of that trouble and I'll help you if you need me."

It was uncanny but he'd just said the same thing that old lady Hattie said to her on the bus the other day.

***

After Terry left she'd taken to the bottle. She must've had at least three or four shots of vodka and she was feeling more relaxed now. Between the shots and the crying, she fell into a deep sleep. She heard the phone ring a couple of times but made no attempts to pick up. She didn't want to speak to anyone. Besides, it was probably for Terry anyway.

Speaking of Terry, where had he gone? He claimed he was going to work but Jordan knew better. She didn't even want to address it anymore. Whatever he did was his business. She had her own problems.

Jordan got out of bed and walked to the kitchen, stumbling over everything in her path and even not in her path. She was that drunk. She wasn't a big drinker so the shots had really affected her. As a matter of fact, the last time she had drank like this was with Trent. That was the night they had first slept together.

Tears welled up in her eyes again. She got out of bed and walked to the answering machine. They had four messages. She pressed the play button.

"Hey, Terry, baby. What's up?"

She hit the skip button.

Next message.

"Hey, Terry, you didn't call me."

Skip.

"Ms. Overton. This is Detective Ross and I need to speak with you. Please call me ASAP."

Well, at least he was still calling me, Jordan jokingly thought to herself. She had to face him at some point. She might as well get it over with.

The last message was a complete surprise.

"Hi, baby. I'm sorry but I got caught up at work tonight and won't be able to go out for dinner as I promised." She heard a muffled noise as if Trent were trying to cover up the receiver of the phone. "Anyway," the message continued, "I'll just see you at work tomorrow and Jordan... I love you."

Jordan turned and quickly ran to the bathroom, bent over the toilet and threw up. The sickness could've been due to the vodka but somehow she doubted it. There were other things making her sicker.

❋❋❋

When Jordan looked at the clock, it read ten. She had fallen asleep—slash—passed out for at least another hour and someone was frantically banging at her door, practically knocking it down.

She scrambled out of bed and made her way to the front door and opened it up.

Trent shuffled past her. "Hey, hon."

Jordan couldn't believe it. *What the hell is he doing here? Shouldn't he be with his sparring partner Charlotte?*

"I just came by to see how you were doing." He narrowed his eyes and studied her with suspicion. "You all right?"

What should she say? She wasn't ready to confront him just yet.

"I'm fine." She uneasily distributed her weight from her right foot to her left and looked down at the ground.

He smirked. "Now, why don't I believe that?"

Jordan looked up at Trent and his arms crossed his chest like teacher awaiting a reply from a reprimanded schoolgirl.

"I just fell asleep and I'm a little tired."

"Really?"

What was with the forty questions?

"Yes, Trent. Really."

He seemed satisfied with that answer.

"You know what I meant to ask you?" He walked closer toward her. "I noticed when you left earlier you forgot your purse."

Damn, she had forgotten about her purse. She glanced over at the dining room table where it was sitting in plain sight.

"So I put it up for you. But later on, I didn't see it anywhere." He walked up closer to her and now stood directly in front of her. "You didn't happen to come back and get it, did you?"

His face was now right in front of hers. He was so close she could smell the sweet-smelling perfume on him. It was strong. Charlotte's, no doubt. He didn't even bother to wash it off before coming to see her.

"No. I didn't come back." She said this a little too quickly. "Maybe someone else took it out of your office. Was there anyone else in your office today, after I left?"

Now she was waiting for his response.

He backed off. "No. No one came in after you," he lied. "So anyway," he said, changing the subject. "I wanted to go out to a late dinner and then you could spend the night at my place. You know, spend some time together?"

Jordan had to come up with an excuse, and fast. There was no way in hell she was going to spend any time with him. "You know, I'm really tired tonight and I have to go to work in the morning."

He put his hands on her waist and kissed her cheek. The perfume was pungent and combined with the smell of sex. *What the heck was he doing to get this scent all over him as it was?* The mere thought sickened her. She couldn't believe he didn't smell it himself.

"You don't have to go to work in the morning." He grinned at her. "Remember, I'm the boss and I order you to take a day off."

Oh, why doesn't he just go home and leave me alone?

She wanted to slap him in the face and leave him stunned but instead she forced a smile.

"I want to go to work, sweetheart." She gently brushed his arm with the tips of her fingers. "Besides, I have those invoices I have to get out by tomorrow. If I don't do it, who will?"

"I could get Charlotte to do it."

Yeah, he could get Charlotte to do a lot of things.

"No, I really want to get those out myself. Besides, I figured I'd come over tomorrow and hang out."

She hoped the promise of tomorrow would be enough to put him off today.

"Fine. I can see you are intent on sending out those invoices, so I'll just wait until tomorrow."

He turned and started to walk toward the front door.

Damn! He had to walk past the dining room table. She wanted to leap for the purse and throw it into the kitchen but it would be too obvious. She walked up ahead of him and turned to face him in order to divert his attention.

Trent's voice altered to a playful erotic tone. "Yes, may I help you?"

"I just wanted to say that I can't wait until tomorrow."

Jordan swallowed hard and slowly brought her lips to his and kissed him. He took it a step further and inserted his tongue, which almost made her sick again, right there in his mouth. This was the same mouth that he had done Lord-knows-what with Charlotte.

"See you tomorrow then." He walked out the door.

Jordan slammed the door shut and ran to the bathroom to literally wash her mouth out with soap.

CHAPTER 31

ordan sat at her desk at work and debated on whether or not she should call Detective Ross and explain everything to him. She had tried to call him the previous night after Trent left but he wasn't in the office. Oddly enough, no one answered so she couldn't even leave a message. She wanted to go down to the police station and attempt to clear her name in person, but she really had no idea how to go about doing so. Why would they even believe her now?

She would wait. She wouldn't call him until she had more answers. But if she waited too long, he would eventually come searching for her and that wouldn't look too good.

"Beep."

Jordan hoped that wasn't him on the phone. She looked down at the number and it was an internal call.

"Hey," the voice said after she picked up.

"Hey."

The voice sounded familiar but she was unsure who it was.

"You wanna go to lunch today, my treat?" It was Gerald.

"Oh, hey, Gerald. I can't today. I'm really busy."

"Oh, c'mon, you need a break. Besides, Mr. Prescott isn't coming in today so we can stay out all afternoon if we want to."

How in the hell did he know this and if it was true, why wasn'
Trent coming in today and more importantly, why didn't he tell her
this yesterday?

Gerald always knew things that no one else knew. Jordan didn'
bother to ask because she would get the "connections, baby
connections" line again.

"Yeah, I know he won't be here." She was lying. This was new
to her.

Gerald was speechless. "How did you know he was going to be
out of town for the next three days?" She heard desperation in hi
voice.

Three days?!?!? He'd said nothing of the sort to her. She wondered
if Charlotte knew.

"Hellooo? I am his secretary. I know things, too," she said lying
again. It was just becoming too easy for her.

Gerald was silent. It was as if she had completely stunned him
with her faux knowledge of Trent's whereabouts.

"Anyway," he said slowly. " I think we should go out to lunch and
BOO-YA, stay out all afternoon until it's time to go home."

Jordan almost dropped the phone. It hit her like a ton of bricks
He was the voice she'd heard on the phone talking to Trent. Gerald
was the one. He was in on it. Whatever *it* was. She didn't recognize
it at first because he never called her. He always just came down
and harassed her.

"Helllooooooo?" he said annoyed.

"Oh, yeah. Let's go to lunch today. Meet me in the lobby at one."
She tried to sound as casual as possible but she was still stunned
upon her realization.

"Meet ya then." Gerald hung up.

Jordan picked up the phone and dialed Charlotte's extension.

"Good morning, Mr. Trent Prescott's office."

Slut.

Jordan mustered up her cheeriest voice. "Good morning, Charlotte, it's Jordan."

"Why hello, Jordan. What can I do for you?"

Phony, phony, phony.

"I know Trent is out of the office for the next three days but he didn't leave me a forwarding number. I need to get in contact with him right away."

"Uh, *you* know he's out of the office?" Charlotte seemed shocked by this news.

Why was everyone so shocked that she would know her so-called fiancé's whereabouts?

"Yes, but he didn't leave a number where I could reach him."

Charlotte's voice got chilly with a snotty edge to it. "He didn't leave a forwarding number since he'll be out of the country. He gave strict instructions he is not to be contacted until he returns."

So if we have questions, how are we to reach him? You at least have to have his number. Maybe you could contact him for me?" Jordan wanted to know if Charlotte was able to get in contact with him at all.

"No. Even *I* don't have a number. I am not to contact him either. If you have any business concerns, you are to contact Jack Marsden."

"Thanks anyway." Jordan quickly hung up.

Charlotte could've been lying but she didn't think so. She was nothing more than his playpen partner, just as she, herself had been. In fact, Jordan was certain Charlotte was kept in the dark just as much as she was. Then again, Charlotte at least knew he was leaving town for a few days. She figured, on the jackass scale, Charlotte was a little further up than she. On the flip side, she had this sham of a ring so that probably made them about equal.

If Trent had given her this ring, she wondered what he had given to Charlotte.

***

"Gerald, could you meet me down here instead of in the lobby?" Jordan had called Gerald to confirm their lunch date.

"No prob. Why?"

"I just need help moving these boxes Trent asked me to get rid of."

"Sure, I'll be down at one."

"Cool."

Jordan was still in shock from the recollection of his voice on that phone call. The way he had ridiculed her along with Trent made her livid. He had told Trent that he needed to take care of her. What exactly did that mean? She was planning on finding out, and that asshole Gerald was going to be the one to tell her, but first she had to take care of him.

At twelve forty-five, Jordan called upstairs to Tracey, one of her coworkers. Her cube was adjacent to Gerald's and she could see him from where she sat.

"Hey, girl," Tracey said upon hearing her voice.

"Hey, Tracey. Gerald's meeting me down here to go to lunch. Could you call me before he leaves? I have to print out something for him before he comes down and I want it ready by the time he gets here."

"Sure thing."

Tracey was the type of woman that was always cheery and never had anything bad to say against someone else. Jordan liked her. Come to think of it, she was pretty much the only person she liked in this office aside from one or two others. Tracey did her work and minded her business.

At eleven-thirty her phone rang again. She looked at the display. It was an outside call. She didn't want to answer it for fear that it would be Detective Ross. She wanted to be the one to contact him. She just needed a little more time. She picked it up anyway and if it wasn't him, she made up her mind to call him and tell him she could meet him at the station the following night. Hopefully, she would have more to go on by then.

"PHC, Industries, may I help you?" She used her most pleasant business voice. She purposely didn't give her name. If it was Detective Ross, she could feign like she was another person and pretend to take a message. This could buy her more time.

"Jordan? Is that you?" Terry said.

"Terry? What's up?"

"I just wanted to make sure you were okay. I didn't see you anymore last night and when I came in this morning, you had already left and I saw a half-empty bottle of vodka on the kitchen table."

"I'm fine but I still don't know what to do."

"You need to go to the police." He was insistent on this and made no secret of it either.

She sighed. "I know but I think I have some new information. Besides, if they really wanted to talk to me ASAP, they could've hunted me down here. It's not like I'm hiding or anything."

"Whatever. But when you come home, we are going to the police. I don't even know why you're still working there. You're not safe. If Mr. Boss Man was willing to set you up, then he could be willing to do anything."

Terry just had no idea. She'd never told him about the "take care of it" comment or even about Mrs. Prescott's untimely death. She also wasn't ready to tell him about Gerald yet. She wanted to follow this lead before she said anything to anyone, including Terry.

A thought came to her. In the office the previous day, Trent had mentioned something about Hines and Jacquie being out of the picture.

How did he know Jacquie was out of the picture? She hadn't said anything regarding her demise.

"Jordan, have you really thought about this?" Terry interrupted her thoughts.

"What do you mean?"

"It's not just that he set you up for the fall. The question is why would he set you up."

"What?" She was confused.

"Think about it. Why would he go through all of this to set you up if he was an innocent man?"

Jordan knew exactly what Terry was saying. There was no other reason for Trent to set her up. Trent had to have murdered Hines or at least played some part in it.

CHAPTER 32

I t was twelve forty-eight and Jordan hadn't gotten a call from Tracey yet. Gerald had a habit of loitering around the office for an hour or two until he actually left the building for lunch. She figured Tracey might have missed him. At one-ten she started to get worried. Maybe he changed his mind or maybe he was on his way now and Tracey forgot to call.

"Beep."

It was internal.

"Hey, Jordan," Tracey said cheerfully as she picked up. "He's grabbing his keys and leaving now."

"Thanks, Tracey. Now I can hurry up and print this stuff out." She wanted to reiterate that so there was nothing to question.

"You know, we should go to lunch someday," Tracey said in her customary high-spirited manner.

That wasn't an invitation to converse.

"Yeah, I'll call you," Jordan said and hung up.

＊＊＊

Gerald walked into the elevator and pressed the down arrow. When it reached the second floor he stepped off and looked down the hall and saw Jordan on the phone with her back turned to him. He casually strolled toward her desk, inadvertently hearing a piece of her conversation.

"Trent, I know, but it's going to be difficult and when exactly are you coming back?" she said into the receiver.

Gerald took two steps back and stood as silent as a lion about to pounce on its prey. He keenly listened to her on the phone. No movement at all.

"Trent, I don't know if I can do this. He's a friend of mine and I like him. We need to rethink this before we do anything rash."

Gerald took a few more steps backward and was now directly in front of the opened elevator. If Jordan turned around, he would be able to act like he had just come down to meet her for lunch.

"Okay, honey, I love you, too." Jordan kissed the phone and then hung up.

Before she could swivel around in her chair, Gerald jumped back into the elevator and pressed the "close" button. Once he was sure it was okay, he opened the doors and walked out to Jordan, sitting facing the elevator. She was off the phone.

"Hey, Gerald." She tried mimicking Tracey's tone. "I can't wait for lunch. I'm starving."

"Uh-yea, let's go." He stopped in his tracks and turned back to her. "By the way, where are the boxes you wanted me to help out with?"

Jordan smiled. "It's all being taken care of."

CHAPTER 33

"Dang, girl, where did you get that ring?"

Gerald took her to Friday's for lunch and as they sat there eating, Jordan wanted to take her fork and shove it down his throat. She didn't want to be anywhere near his disgusting presence, but she had to keep up the façade if she was to find out any more information.

"Gerald, you mean to tell me that you don't know?"

She enjoyed watching him make a fool out of himself. She knew good and well he knew about the ring.

"Don't know what?" He took a huge bite of his big fat greasy burger. Ketchup spilled out the other end, making a big splash onto his plate.

This guy was unbelievable. Unbelievable and a bad actor.

"Hmmm, I guess you wouldn't know," she said slyly.

"Know what?"

"Trent and I are getting married!"

Those words were the most difficult words she'd ever had to speak; even though she knew the entire thing was fake.

Gerald pretended to choke on the huge bite he had in his mouth. He grabbed his napkin and spit it out in one large, mushy clump. Jordan wanted to laugh. He was really going all out with this charade.

"Say again?" He pounded on his chest with his fist, clearing his throat.

"Trent and I are getting married." Again, she attempted to act as though this was the happiest news in the world rather than news that was bound to bring up her lunch.

"That's great." He took a sip of water. "That's really great."

He provided her with all that visual with the spitting out the burger but now that's all he had to say? Well, if he couldn't play it right, she knew how.

"Aren't you even surprised that Trent and I are dating?"

He took another sip of water, no doubt trying to stall so he could figure out how to respond. "Of course, I'm surprised. I had no idea."

She almost laughed out loud. She could've put him up against the wall some more but why bother? It was time to go in for the kill. She wanted to break down this bond he and Trent shared. If Gerald felt suspicious about Trent, he might help her out but she had to work fast. She only had three days.

"Gerald?" She grabbed his hand from across the table. "You know I really value our friendship."

Gerald looked at Jordan with such a confused expression that she knew she was going to enjoy this more than she had originally anticipated.

"I can't get into it now. I really need to talk to you but I can't do it here."

"What is it?" He was literally on the edge of his seat.

"If you can, we should go out for a drink tonight. Trent and I have been talking about a few things and I think you should be in on it."

"What? What things have you guys been talking about?" His voice was in a panic.

This was heaven.

"Not now. Tonight."

Gerald finally relented and told Jordan that he would meet her for drinks.

They were in the car and headed back to the office. He didn't say

word to her. She knew the little wheels in his head were turning
ust as fast as the spinners he had just paid some serious cash for.

*What news could she possibly have for him regarding a discussion
between her and Trent?* She guaranteed that's exactly what he was
hinking.

"Oh, by the way, do you know how I can get in touch with
Prescott?" Gerald was trying hard to sound indifferent.

She wasn't going to let him off that easy. "Why?"

"I just need him to sign some invoices for me."

It was killing Gerald that he couldn't talk to Trent, *if* that was the
case. She took a gamble, not really knowing if Gerald was able to
contact him or not, but from his reaction, he was unreachable to
him also. For some peculiar reason, Trent had really made himself
unavailable to everyone.

"Oh, don't worry about that. You can take them down to Jack
Marsden. He'll be signing the invoices until Trent comes back."

"Okay, thanks."

Gerald grew silent again. She knew he'd attempt another way to
get the information from her. If not her, she guaranteed he'd go
right to Charlotte and see if she knew how to reach him. She smiled
to herself as she thought about him scrambling around trying to
track Trent down. If he only knew. Jordan had seen Gerald when
he had come down to her desk to pick her up for lunch. She was
actually talking to a dial tone rather than Trent, his partner in
crime, as he suspected. She knew Trent was too smart to be picked
clean for information, but Gerald was a whole 'nother turkey.

✻✻✻

When she got to her desk, she saw the voice mail light lit up on
her phone. *Probably Terry,* she thought, as she pressed the button to
listen to the message.

"Good afternoon, Ms. Overton. This is Detective Michael Ross. I need to get in contact with you as soon as possible. Please give me a call."

He left his number again. She thought about calling him back right away but she had nothing to go on. She would have more information later. She would just put it off until after she came home from milking Gerald for information. If she could come up with something, she could let the police handle the rest.

Twenty minutes later, Gerald came down to her desk and casually took a seat right on the edge as he always did. "Hey, what's up?"

This guy was too obvious. It tickled her to see him squirm but attempt to look cool and collected. Trent he was not.

"Hey, Gerald. What brings you down here? Didn't I just see you?" she said jokingly.

"Nothing. I just wanted to see what's up down here."

"Nothing new. Just trying to get these invoices done before I leave," she said, not looking up from her desk.

"Need help?"

"No, I'm fine."

"Okay then."

He got up off her desk and started walking away.

Asshole.

"Oh, I just remembered." He turned back to her. "I can't go out tonight. I have things to do."

Jordan looked up at him and couldn't resist. "Really? What?"

He didn't expect that question. She saw it on his face. "I got this stupid thing to go to. I totally forgot about it until just now."

"Oh." She was good at sounding disappointed. "We can go out another time then."

She looked down and went back to invoicing. He stood above her. She couldn't see him but she could feel his eyes on her.

"Maybe we should discuss whatever you wanted to talk about now.

He certainly was being aggressive and she knew exactly why.

"Gerald, it's not a big deal. Trent is calling me tonight," she lied. "I want to wait until I talk to him again before saying anything anyway."

"Say anything about what?"

Now he was really nervous. She saw a look of terror in his eyes. They actually began to tear up. This man was scared to death of Trent and she was beginning to wonder if she herself should be more afraid.

"Gerald, calm down."

"What is it?" He was more impatient.

She decided to let him off the hook for fear he would reach across the desk and strangle her until she told him. "It's nothing. I was just going to ask you to be an usher in our wedding."

She saw the look of amazement and then relief on his face.

"Uh, sure." He laughed nervously. "That's what you wanted to talk to me about?"

Her face got serious. "Should there be something else?" She looked him dead in his face and was sure not to blink.

He got nervous all over again. "No."

There was an uneasy silence for a moment. Not uncomfortable for her but for him. She narrowed her eyes, scrutinizing him up and down trying to figure out what it was that he and Trent had going. How long had they been setting her up and was he in on the murder? The guy standing before her sweating bullets was too idiotic to be involved in anything so criminal. Or was he?

✳✳✳

Jordan left the office early that day. She sat on the couch looking out of the window just thinking about everything. She had Gerald wired up now. She wasn't sure how she was going to proceed with this whole thing, but she wanted to see his reaction to her setup that afternoon. He was bound to put two and two together and knowing his dumb ass, he'd come up with five. But she had to bank on the fact that even he'd realize that the conversation he "accidentally overheard" didn't jibe with the whole asking him to be the usher thing. She only had three days to do it because Trent was coming back, and she didn't want those two talking before she had a chance to do what she had to do.

She went into the kitchen to pour another glass of vodka and before she knew it she had three vodkas on the rocks. The sun was setting and it was beginning to get dark. She was lonely and very much afraid. Lately, Terry had been out and she had no clue what he was doing or where he was going. She talked to him on the phone more than she saw him. She wasn't sure what she was doing and she needed Terry to guide her. Sometimes it felt as though she was messing with a fire that was burning beyond her control. But what did she have to lose?

She went into the bathroom and looked at herself in the mirror. She was tired and run down. When she actually thought about it she couldn't believe the mess she was in. The tears ran down her face and she began to cry. She sat right there on the bathroom floor and quietly sobbed. This was all getting beyond her control. She had never felt so alone in her life. It was like she was slowly drowning and there was no one there to pull her out. She just wanted everything to be all right. She wanted to come home from work and complain about Hines. She wanted Terry to annoy her about her weight again. She wanted to watch Trent admiringly from afar and come home and ask Terry how to make her beautiful to impress him. She wanted her old life back.

But all that was gone.

All of the simplicity in her life was replaced by a murder that had evil, deceitful lies attached. She sometimes wished she hadn't overheard Trent talking to Gerald. Would it have been better if she had been blind to the entire thing? Jordan knew better. It was just scar knowing her world had been turned upside-down and she was quite possibly being accused of a murder. As silly as it seemed, she just wanted to rest and close her eyes, pretending it never happened.

Jordan cried and cried until her distended eyes were dried out. She thought about just going to the police and begging them to believe her but she already had dug her own grave by deceiving them. Lying for a man who was setting her up to take the fall. He didn't need to set her up; she was doing an excellent job of that all by herself.

Jordan was upset that she was like a puppet and Trent had pulled all the strings. He knew she would come to his rescue. Save him and drown herself. That's exactly what she had done. She thought Gerald to be a pawn but she was just as much a playing piece as he was.

She cried even harder when she realized that she might be in imminent danger herself. This really scared her. She still didn't know what "take care of her" meant. Was Trent actually planning on doing harm to her?

A knock on the front door made her jump. She'd been sitting on the bathroom floor for an hour and the sun was setting, forming eerie shadows inside the small room. She got up off the floor and went to the door. It was Detective Ross. He had finally caught up with her and she didn't care. She was too fatigued to even think about it anymore.

Once she had the door cracked open, he said, "Good evening." He had a severe look on his face. "May I come in?"

Jordan opened the door wider and walked back to the living room without saying a word and leaving him to shut the door behind himself.

"Are you okay, Jordan?"

She turned to him and smiled torpidly. "Are you taking me to the police station to arrest me?" She felt herself slightly slurring her words.

He eyed the empty bottle of vodka on the living room table.

"Yeah, and?" she asked defiantly. "How dare you come in here and look at me accusingly." She stumbled backward. "Then again, you have the right to look at me accusingly considering I am the accused." She found her flavorless joke amusing and started laughing.

She laughed so hard that she almost fell backward onto the couch. Detective Ross hurried across the room and caught her before she landed right on her backside.

He held her in his arms to steady her. She looked up at him. He was so tall, so handsome. Maybe if she slept with him, she could get off for the murder. She shook her head. Now she was believing she committed a murder. It was the alcohol talking but she couldn't help it.

"Maybe I should come back another time."

"Since when do the police come back another time to arrest someone? Wouldn't that be nice?" She stifled another giggle.

He didn't flinch.

She suddenly got serious. "Detective, what are you doing here?"

He let her go and she sat down on the couch. He followed suit and sat down in the chair across from her. The sun was almost down and she could see the shadow of his face. It was a handsome appearance. The first thing you would notice about his face was his strong jaw line. The dimples were a close second.

"I want you to know that I believe you."

She shook her head to make sure she had heard him correctly. "What did you say?"

"I'm sorry," he said, looking around the room. "It's a little dark in here. Could we turn on some lights?"

Jordan stood up and walked across the room to the light switch and flipped it up.

"Now, repeat what you just said?"

"I believe you. I believed you from the beginning."

This baffled her. She hoped she had heard him right. "What exactly do you believe?"

"I don't believe you killed Hines and I believe you had nothing to do with it."

This made her hysterically happy. To know that there was actually someone out there who believed her story; no matter how full of bullshit it sounded.

"Why? I mean, what happened to make you believe me?" She was beginning to sober up quickly.

"In my profession, we're taught to just go on facts. If I did that, you'd be in jail right now," he said lightheartedly. "But I saw you. I saw your eyes and the way you begged for us to believe you. Your words may have been jumbled and fallacious, but I knew that you didn't do it." She waited for him to say more. "I did some checking on my own and found out a few things about your fiancé."

How in the hell did he know he was her fiancé? Right now that was secondary. She just wanted him to say what he had to say.

"I can't tell you exactly what I found but I can tell you that the change of the PHC Industries contract wasn't done by Hines."

"Who did it then?" Jordan found herself fascinated by this information.

"I don't want to mention names yet, but someone was paid off to forge Hines' signature."

"I don't understand. It still had to be notarized by someone."

"Exactly, and that person was paid off, too."

"According to this specific contract that gave you a piece of the company, if you or any other party are incarcerated and unable to make business decisions, you lose your power, therefore losing your percentage."

"So if I'm in jail, then I lose my percentage?" This was unbelievable. "Who would they go to then?"

"Here's the thing. They would go to the other owners."

She began to fit the pieces together herself. "That would be Trent and Jacquie." She slapped her forehead upon this realization.

"That's correct, but along with being incarcerated, meeting an untimely death would mean that the deceased's percentage would be forfeited also."

So two plus two equaled four. If she was in jail and Jacquie was dead Trent got it all.

"That's odd. Why would something like that be included in a contract?"

"That's what we'd like to know." Detective Ross never took his eyes off her.

"So do you think he had something to do with Jacquie's death?"

"Oh, I know he did. I just can't prove it. We have witnesses stating that Jacquie told them Prescott had practically forced her to go to some shoddy mechanic friend of his to fix her brakes that were acting up."

Jordan stood up out of the chair in disbelief.

"That guy was no doubt paid off, too, and has since mysteriously disappeared," he continued.

She looked down at him. This man was remarkable. She had no doubt that he would be able to help her now.

"The best part, and you'll love this..." He stood up. "He has the ball to have a million-dollar lawsuit against the manufacturers of the car his wife was driving, stating they were at fault for her death." He looked down at the ground and laughed. "Your fiancé is one greedy man."

Jordan frowned. "Please stop calling him that. He's not my fiancé."

He looked at her finger and then back at her. "It doesn't seem that way."

She quickly took off the ring. "I'm only wearing it as a..." She searched for the right word. "I'm only wearing it as a prop, so-to speak."

He squinted. "What do you mean, 'prop'?"

"Nothing, just forget it."

He walked closer to her. "You're not doing anything foolish, are you?"

Jordan turned away from him. She had deceived him enough and didn't want to lie to him again, but she wasn't ready to let him in on t just yet. Even if he did believe her, she wanted to be the one to fix what she had broken.

"He's a very dangerous man, Jordan. He's done things that even you don't know about."

She saw the seriousness in his face.

"Tell me this," she said, changing the subject. "So why doesn't he ust kill me off and get me out of the way? Why is he going through ll of that trouble of setting me up?"

Detective Ross shook his head.

"He killed Hines and that got rid of him. He had to set someone ıp to take the fall. As long as you're in jail, he still gets everything..."

"And because his wife is dead," she said, finishing his thought.

He walked toward her and gently placed his hands on her shoulders. Consider the alternative. You could've been in the car accident nd Jacquie could've been the one set up for Hines' murder."

She turned and looked out at the stunning gray sky illuminated ›y millions of tiny stars. She hadn't thought of it that way. Jacquie ould've been the one being framed for Hines' murder and she vould've been the one that was six feet under. When you looked at t that way, she was the lucky one.

She turned back to him. "We can't let him get away with this."

"Jordan, I'm only telling you this so you don't do anything stupid." Ie walked up to her and grabbed her hand. "Prescott is a dangerous nan. The police are going to handle him."

She wanted to trust him but her future was at stake, not to mention er pride was hurt. She had loved this man with all her heart. She ad dreamt about a future with him. She was reminded of what erry had told her about messing with married men, but even he ouldn't have predicted this.

"So the police believe me, too?

He let go of her hand. "Well, not really. I've been doing this after hours. Technically they took me off this case. That's why Detective Carmichael came to see you the other day. He just acquired a warrant for your arrest and should be knocking on your door in the next twenty-four hours."

A warrant? They were trying to put her in jail? Everything was not all right. She was relying on a detective who was no longer on her case? How would he be able to help her now? Not to mention that in less than twenty-four hours, she was going to be behind bars and even more useless. She had to act and act fast. She couldn't wait for him to come up with information on Trent when she was so close. She had to step it up a notch.

"I'm going to help you. I'm not going to let you go to jail." She was desperate and he knew it. "Just hang in there and I'll get 'em. Don't worry about it."

"With all due respect, detective, I don't know what you can do. You yourself said that he's a very dangerous and tricky man."

"Jordan. We'll get him."

She knew he meant well and he really wanted to help, but she couldn't just do nothing. The *hell* she was going to sit behind bars for a murder she had absolutely nothing to do with.

She was surprised by the backbone that inexplicably surfaced out of nowhere. She was fed up with being Trent's puppet. He had pulled the strings and she had danced like a good little girl. Well that was no more. She was getting angrier now. Her life was on the line by his doing. The only thing she was guilty of was loving and devoting herself to him.

"Do what you can. I don't want to go to jail for something I didn't do."

"I will. Just don't do anything to put yourself in harm's way."

Jordan saw no point in arguing with him. He wasn't going to give her his blessing with what she had to do. At this point, she had nothing to lose.

CHAPTER 34

"So what are you gonna do?"

Terry was sitting on the bed next to Jordan drinking a cup of tea. She, on the other hand, had a glass of vodka straight-up.

"I'm going to get Gerald to admit to everything. Right now, he's my only hope. I figure I can take a recorder with me and tape everything. Once he confesses, I can take it to Detective Ross."

"What makes you think you can get him to admit to everything? Didn't you just tell me that he's afraid of Prescott?"

Jordan took a sip from the glass. This was her second drink and nothing was numbing her nerves. "He's the only hope I have. Without him, I'll be put away forever."

Tears stung her eyes as the words escaped her lips and she actually thought about it. There was a possibility she would spend the rest of life behind bars if Gerald didn't help her.

"Are you even going to let Detective Ross in on your plan?"

"I can't. He would just tell me to sit tight and everything will be okay."

Terry stood up. "I still don't like the idea of you trying to play policewoman."

"Terry, what choice do I have? Tell me that."

She waited for a response. Any response. She really did want an answer to that question. She wished Terry would speak magical words that would make everything go away but she knew better. She was well aware of the fact that she had no other alternative. It was this or jail.

Take your pick. And so she chose.

CHAPTER 35

I t was Friday evening and she had skipped work that day. She wanted everything to seem normal but the truth was she was scared to even go back into that place. Although, on the outside, Gerald appeared to be obtuse. Jordan had no way of knowing what he was capable of.

She had called him earlier in the day and told him to meet her after work at the Italian restaurant they had gone to for lunch a while back. That was the same day they had seen Hines and Mrs. Prescott together. Jordan walked in the door and looked around in the crowded restaurant for Gerald. She didn't see him, so she sat at the bar and ordered a vodka tonic. Lately she had been drinking so much and it was taking its toll on her. She wasn't able to sleep at all at night and she was restless all day long. The fact that she was being framed for a murder didn't help either.

Jordan turned around and looked toward the door again. No Gerald. She wished she had a cigarette now. Two minutes later Gerald walked through the door and immediately spotted Jordan at the bar.

"Hey, what's up?" he asked, shouting over the crowd.

"Gerald, I don't have time to play games. I need to talk to you now."

He took a seat next to her. She knew she had his attention. About?"

"I don't know what Trent is offering you, but you can't do this."

"Do what?" He was really acting like he knew nothing.

Jordan realized that she forgotten to turn on the tape recorder. She reached into her pocket and fumbled around for the record button. Her hands trembled with nerves.

He looked down at her shuffling around in the pocket. "What are you doing?"

This was a total disaster. He was going to catch her and never admit to anything and off to jail she would go.

"I'm just looking for my keys," she said nervously.

"What?"

"I said I'm just looking for my keys!" she said louder.

She didn't realize the crowd was going to be so big that night. There was no way she would be able to tape anything he admitted to.

"Oh!" he yelled.

She looked around for a quiet table in the restaurant. She should've known better. This was never going to work. Happy hour on a Friday night.

"Gerald, do you want to go to another restaurant? This one is too crowded."

He nodded and they got up to leave. "My car is right outside." He steered her out the door and toward his car across the street.

They sat silently for a moment in the vehicle. Since Gerald was driving, it was a little easier for Jordan to find the record button in her right side pocket without him noticing.

"I left something at the office. Do you mind?" he asked.

Jordan shook her head. This might even be a little better for her. This way the recorder would catch everything.

Gerald drove all the way to the office without saying a word. Jordan was too edgy to say anything to him. When they reached the office, he told her to come up because he might be a little while.

They got to his desk and he turned on his computer and fiddled with some papers, appearing somewhat anxious. "You know, I can never get all of my work done."

Jordan nodded without saying a word.

"What was it you wanted to talk to me about?" He started walking toward her.

"What? Oh, that. Nothing." Jordan's hands were shaking with fright. She wasn't sure how to bring it up now. She could just blurt it out, but what would his reaction be? If she really thought about it, she would never say anything. She needed more time. Why hadn't she planned this better? She closed her eyes tightly and thought about prison being her home for the rest of her life.

"I know something's going on. I know everything. Trent told me what you two were planning."

Gerald looked up from his desk. "What do you mean?"

She took a deep breath and continued. "I know everything. Trent came to me the other day and told me."

Gerald took another step toward her as she took two steps back. "What do you know?"

"Everything."

"Jordan, I have no idea what you're talking about."

She reached into her pocket to make sure she had the record button pressed.

"What do you have in your pocket?" He looked down.

Her cover was blown. He would never confess to anything now. She looked around and realized they were alone. It was Friday after hours so no one was going to be in the office. Like a snare drum, her heart beat grew faster when she remembered that the cleaning people didn't work Friday evenings. They were completely alone. She'd been so edgy she didn't realize that she had put herself in a position riddled with danger.

Gerald took another step toward her. In an instant Jordan turned and ran down the hall. Instead of heading for the elevator, she made a dash for the steps, taking them two at a time, almost stumbling to the hard cement ground.

When she got to the lobby, she sprinted toward the main doors and bolted out like lightning. As she rapidly ran down the sidewalk, she turned around to make sure he wasn't behind her. When she saw she was in the clear, she slowed down to a brisk walk. She couldn't have anticipated what had just happened. She couldn't take it anymore. This was just too much for her. She tried to be strong and clear her name on her own, but she couldn't do it. She would just have to rely on Detective Ross. After all, he was a detective. If he couldn't do it, no one could. She had had enough.

CHAPTER 36

"What happened to you?"

When she got home, Terry was waiting for her. He took one look at her disheveled clothes and came to her with concern.

She held up her hands and shook her head. She didn't want to talk about it. If she told him just how scared she was, he would only say "I told you so." No matter the situation, you could count on an "I told you so" from Terry, and this was just not the time.

"Detective Ross just called." The look of alarm remained on his face. "He left his number for you to call him back."

Jordan hoped he had good news. He would have to act fast considering she had just blown it with Gerald. It was lucky that Trent was still out of town and Gerald couldn't contact him. She was sure the first chance he got, he would tell him everything. What really scared her was now they might come after her if they thought she really did know everything. She had messed up badly.

She dialed the number on the napkin Terry had written the message on. When someone picked up, she realized it was a residence. She hung up the phone and dialed again. Maybe she had misdialed, but again, the same voice answered the phone.

"Terry, you took down the wrong number," she said in exaspertion.

He grabbed it from her hand and looked at it. "Just call information and they can give you the police department's number."

When she got the number from 411, she quickly dialed. It was now time to let Detective Ross know what had happened and what she had been planning. Hopefully he would be able to rectify her mess.

"Just a minute," the operator said. A minute later she returned "Which department?"

Which department? She hadn't the foggiest. She hung up the phone retreated to her room and turned her purse upside-down on her bed. At the very bottom, she found the card with his number. On the back, he had written another number for the police department.

Thank goodness.

When she dialed the number, she let it ring over and over and over, but no one answered. She hung up and started to dial again when Terry knocked on her bedroom door.

"Jordan, Detective Ross is here to see you."

She hung up the phone in relief and walked out to the living room to meet him. "I was just trying to call you."

"Prescott is back in town." There was urgency in his voice. "I need you to do me a big favor and it may be taking a risk but we have to nail this guy now. I just found out he plans on leaving town again."

Jordan felt her heart in her throat. He was back in town? He probably had already talked to Gerald. If so, what were they planning for her now?

"Detective, I have to tell you something."

"Not now, Jordan. You have to get him to admit to everything."

"Detective, I tried that and..."

"You have to talk to him *now* and get him to admit to everything," he repeated

Terry stepped up. "There is no way she's going to put herself i jeopardy. That's you guys' job, not hers."

"It's okay. The police believe you and we've set up a sting operation His office is already bugged."

"He's at the office?" she asked.

"Yes. He's there now. Don't worry; the place is crawling with cops."

When she didn't move, he spoke up again. "If we don't do this now, they'll be no way we can ever catch this guy. He'll get away with this and you'll go to jail for the rest of your life. Maybe even get the death penalty."

Frenziedly, Jordan started crying. She didn't know what to do. She hadn't expected to have to confront him so soon. She was more scared of him than she thought. Even though the police were going to be there, she still didn't feel completely safe. She needed more time.

"You've got to go now. Before he leaves." Detective Ross grabbed her hand and led her to the front door.

She had to get herself together. She couldn't mess up like she had done with Gerald. This was her last and final chance. If this didn't work, she didn't know what she was going to do next.

CHAPTER 37

She walked toward his office and saw the light on through the bottom of the door. The door was shut but she was able to see a shadow flit recklessly back and forth.

There was a crash of something behind the door. Then silence. The shadow continued to move heedlessly, unaware that someone was standing outside the door.

She looked around wondering exactly where the police were hidden. The place seemed completely desolate. She thought about knocking but decided against it. It would be better to catch him off guard.

Warily, she opened the door and stood in the doorway, not making a sound. She observed Trent moving swiftly from his desk to his corporate bathroom and then to his closet. He was completely oblivious that someone was standing there watching him.

"Trent?"

With trepidation, he dropped the large box he had in his hand.

"What are you doing here?"

"Trent, I know everything."

As soon as the words had escaped her lips, she realized that was the same line she had used for Gerald and it hadn't worked then.

"Jordan, you need to get out of here and as soon as possible." He was barely listening to her. He was rambling on with what he had to say. "If you don't, you could be in trouble, too."

He inexorably scurried around not realizing a single word she spoke.

"Trent, I know what you're doing."

"Doing? The only thing I'm doing is trying to get the hell outta here before it's too late." He put some more papers and books into the box, then reached behind him and into a file cabinet. "I'd advise you to do the same."

Getting him to admit to the murders wasn't going to be an effortless task but by this time, she didn't fear him at all. He was so preoccupied with getting out of town before the police caught up with him. He barely noticed her.

"Trent, I know you killed Hines and I know why."

This caught his attention. He peered up from the boxes and started laughing. "What the hell are you talking about? Are you mad?"

"Don't deny it." She steadied herself. "The police told me everything."

"Are you referring to Jeremy? I assure you, if he told you something it was a lie."

Who was Jeremy?

"Why did you kill him?"

"Kill who?" he asked with an elevated degree of asperity in his voice.

Despite her desire to have him admit to everything, she could see that he was going to be obdurate about it.

"Hines. You killed him," she repeated.

He continued with packing boxes. "I didn't kill Hines."

"What about Jacquie?"

"What about her?" he said, not looking up.

Wherever he was going, he wanted to get there quickly.

"Why did you kill her then?"

Trent made a roaring noise that made her jump. "I didn't kill anyone. You're barking up the wrong tree."

"Then why did you set me up? Why did you have me lie to the police about your whereabouts the night of Hines' murder?"

He ran into the bathroom and got a few more things.

Is he even listening to me?

"Jordan, I asked you to lie for me because I'm involved in something illegal. I have been running an ecstasy ring and that's where I was that night. I needed you to lie so the police wouldn't catch up with me."

She didn't know what to say. Was he lying? She couldn't tell anymore.

"If that's true, you'd rather go to jail for murder than on a drug charge? That doesn't make sense."

"No, I'd rather not go to jail on any charge. It was supposed to be that way but everything fell apart and now it's gotten much worse than just going to jail."

"What about Charlotte?"

He clandestinely smiled. "I knew you came back for your purse," he said calmly.

"You'd been sleeping with her."

"So? I was cheating on my wife with you and on you with Charlotte. That doesn't make me a murderer, just an asshole."

"So why are you packing up and leaving if you didn't commit the murders?"

Exasperated, he sat down in his leather chair. "Sweet, innocent Jordan. You have no idea what you're involved in." He pitifully shook his head at her. "Everything wasn't adding up. It looked like I was the murderer. I thought it was the police that may have been setting me up but I had no idea why. When I found out Jacquie had been killed, I couldn't figure out what was going on."

"And your lawsuit with the manufacturers of her car?"

He looked at her with surprise. "What the fuck are you talking about?"

He inhaled deeply and pivoted around in the chair to gaze out his window. It was like he had just then given up on escaping from whatever or whoever was after him, as he so frenetically put it.

"I hired a private investigator and do you know what he told me?"

Her head was still whirring from what he just told her before
She couldn't imagine. "No."

Still facing the window, he looked up at the ceiling in anguish and
sighed again.

"He told me that someone from my past was setting me up."

"Setting you up? Why?"

He stood up and turned around to face her.

"My dear, business is a bitch. Never backstab the wrong person
because it will come back and bite you in the ass."

"What does this have to do with me?"

She forgot why she had come here in the first place. She was supposed to be getting him to admit to the murders but in actuality she
had done the exact opposite. He had denied everything. What he
was talking about now wasn't making any sense at all.

"Unfortunately, you're the fall guy—or girl, if you will." He
laughed. It seemed he still had his sense of humor. "If I were you
I'd start packing my things because Jeremy is spiteful. Just ask my
man Billy and Jacquie." He chortled malevolently. "Oh, wait, you
can't unless you have a shovel and a high tolerance for badly
decomposed dead bodies."

She ignored his repugnant sense of humor. "Who is Jeremy?"

Just then she heard a loud pop. She turned to the door but saw no
one. When she turned back around, Trent stood there with his
mouth gaped open and his eyes bulging in horror.

He collapsed into the leather chair behind him and made no
more movement. The front of his white shirt was beginning to get
saturated with a deep red stain that was getting larger and larger.

"Trent?!?!" Jordan screamed but he didn't answer.

Just then she heard a voice behind her. "You wanted to know who
Jeremy is? Well, here I am."

CHAPTER 38

She recognized the voice. She slowly turned back to the door to face the person who was speaking.

"Detective Ross?" She was breathless.

"Oh, come now. Don't tell me you're surprised. I was good but not *that* good."

Detective Ross stood in the doorway ensconced in black from head to toe, including a pair of black leather gloves. The face she had once trusted was now fraught with guile. She couldn't speak.

"Well, from the looks of it, maybe I did completely surprise you." He had unwavering grandiosity in his tone as he grinned at her. "Allow me to introduce myself. My name is Jeremy Culmer."

He raised one gloved hand that was behind his back and held it out to her from across the room. "Nice to meet you," he said, laughing. He lowered his hand and took a step closer to her. He reached back to shut the door and lock it. "I suppose about now you're wondering what the hell is going on."

The temerity in his voice indicated he knew exactly what was going on and was about to let her in on his furtive dementia.

"I had this all mapped out. I calculated this moment for years and all it took was a bit of rudimentary police work, and I was well on my way to executing the master plan."

She looked around the room for any way out but she was trapped. Caught inside this office with a madman.

"You don't know how much preparation I had to go through to bring this to life. It took years to get to this point, and I loved every minute of it knowing what the end result would be." He propelled himself a little closer. "Killing Hines was the best, as of yet. I had no idea succinylcholine worked that fast." He wrapped his hands around his neck and squeezed it in a mock chokehold. "You should've seen the expression on his face. That asshole knew he was going to die. know it. It was pure heaven."

He looked up into the sky with a wily smile on his face, fondly remembering every single squalid infinitesimal detail of his crime. "Not to mention beautiful, wonderful Jacquelyn Prescott, my ex-wife."

His ex-wife?

The expression on his face turned to one of anger. "Now that wasn't as pleasurable. I didn't get to see the look on that bitch's face as she died." He shifted his eyes to her. "But I can just imagine the horror she must've felt when she plunged to her death. Can you imagine that, Jordan?" he asked excitedly. "The sheer terror of pressing your brakes and nothing happening."

He smiled to himself as he thought about it. He was truly enjoying this.

"I don't understand, detective. Why?" She asked, partially because she wanted to know and also because she wanted to buy time. She imagined she wasn't going to fare much better with the fate he had in store for her.

"Oh, I guess you haven't figured it out yet, but I'm no detective. thought you could've figured that out but luckily for me, you're denser than I thought."

"But, I called the police station for you a couple of times."

"No, you called the number on the card I gave you. Let's just say have friends who owe me favors."

"You are absolutely crazy. You know that?!" she screamed. "You're not going to get away with this. There is no way in hell you're going to get away with this."

"Insane? I don't think so. In fact, I'm completely lucid right now. I've gotten away with it so far, haven't I? Let me see, I killed Hines and fixed it so you and Trent were the main suspects. How slick was that? I couldn't have done it better myself." He looked past her and at the lifeless body in the leather chair. "Oops, I guess Trent is out of that running now. Oh, and there's Jacquie who was in a terrible 'accident.'" He frowned as he mocked disappointment. "Poor thing."

He casually took another step closer.

"So my guess is that you are now the number one suspect."

"You won't get away with this. There's no way. Once I tell the police everything, they'll investigate you and figure out it was you!" she screamed.

The sinister look in his eyes heightened.

"That is precisely why this will be a murder suicide." He took one more step closer. He was slowly easing his way toward her and she had no place to go. "I even had the PHC contract changed so that you would hold a percentage. That really made you look like a suspect." He laughed out loud. "Those idiots bought it, too. I thought that was going to be tricky but it was simple."

She had a bizarre feeling of vertigo. Her feet were tenuously situated on the grainy carpet. What was she going to do?

"But why? Why did you do it? What did I do to you? I didn't even know you. I trusted you."

"Oh, don't give me that pitiful bullshit. I must say, I do find you attractive but in order to carry out my plan, I had to make someone the pigeon. Isn't that the word your dead fiancé used? Pigeon?"

How did he know that?

"You're probably wondering how I knew that." It was as if he was reading her mind. "As a matter of fact I contrived this whole thing with Trent's secretary in mind, but when you came to work here a few months ago, I knew you were the one. Especially with the great chemistry you and Hines had."

He snickered at her. "And you thought Trent here was the murderer and that his lackey Gerald was in on it."

He laughed so hard it made her angry. How did he know all of this? He must've been watching her or quite possibly had her apartment bugged. Her mind raced as she thought about the different scenarios.

"Now that was classic." He calmed himself down and wiped away the tears he had in his eyes from his self-amusement.

This would be the time to try to get away but her legs were frozen in the spot where she stood. She didn't want to die.

"The best part was you trying to set up Gerald and Trent against each other. Now that was funny. They had no idea what you were talking about. They just thought you were crazy."

He bent over and slapped his knees while laughing uncontrollably. She couldn't believe he was laughing as hard as he was, right after he had just shot someone and planned on killing her.

This was her chance. She had to take it. She grabbed the metallic souvenir globe Trent had on his desk and ran toward him full force. Before she knew it, with all of her strength, she rammed it into his stomach and knocked him over. A massive *UMMPH* sound emerged deep from within his diaphragm as he doubled over in pain. The gun he had in his hand flew up into the air and toward her desk situated outside the office.

As she attempted to step over his fallen body, he grabbed her ankle and twisted it. With a loud thud, she fell to the ground, bumping her head. Blood trickled down her smarting temple.

She kicked at him, aiming for his testicles, but got his thigh instead. He squirmed his way on top of her and put his large, sturdy hand over her mouth, keeping her from making a sound. She twisted and turned but could barely move. The more she twisted, the more he threw his body weight on top of her. He was just too heavy for her frame. He removed his hand from her mouth and put it on her neck squeezing tightly until it cut off her airway. She scrambled as hard as she could, realizing it would take nothing short of a miracle for her to free herself from his strong grasp. With his other hand, he reached for a black leather bag that was inches from her head. Once he got it, he pulled out a sinewy looped piece of rope. It was a noose. He was going to hang her from it, making it look as though she had committed suicide.

She kicked and scrambled with less force. His hand around her throat was sucking the air from her lungs. With much difficulty, he was able to place the rope around her neck and drag her back into the office, forcefully slamming her onto the desk like a rag doll. She tried to scream but the noose was just too tight and blocking her airway. The more she tried, the more oxygen she lost. She was getting light-headed.

He took the straight end of the rope and slung it over a beam in the office. She looked around in a panic for anything. She saw letter openers, scissors, rulers, pencils, but they were all out of her reach. She looked over at Trent, who twitched in his chair. He was alive! He could help her.

As he started to pull the rope, making her head rise up from the desk, she glanced at Trent again. This time there was no movement and his face was as ashen as a specter. The lack of oxygen was making her hallucinate.

She felt the air abscond her body as quickly as if she had been blowing it out herself. She still had some fight in her but she kicked and twisted to no avail. As it got tighter and tighter, the makeshift noose seared a mark into her neck.

She envisioned someone coming into the office the next morning and finding the bodies as she herself had found Hines on that atrocious day. The sight would be indelibly imprinted into their minds as Hines had been in hers.

Only she couldn't remember that day anymore. She couldn't remember any of the unpleasant events that had recently taken place. She wafted in and out of consciousness until all she saw was complete stillness.

CHAPTER 39

Gazing around the room in a fog, she noticed it was completely unblemished, spotless from corner to corner. She figured she must have been in the hospital because everything was so white and crisp and smelled of disinfectant. Just like her dreams. There was even a chilly draft coming in from... Where was this draft coming from?

Up ahead she saw Trent and she called to him but he was too far away to hear her. In fact, no one was around to hear her. The tiny room contained only a chair, and its entranceway had a door that was wide open. That enabled her to see outside the room.

She was getting a little cold now. She wished someone would bring her a blanket. But no one in the entranceway was paying her any attention. Not even her mother.

Her mother?

She hadn't seen her mother in years. Come to think of it, why not? She never called either. She would have to make it a point to call her again and have lunch.

"Jordan?"

Someone was speaking to her but she saw no one. Her eyes were shut.

Slowly, she opened them up and saw Terry.

"Jordan. Are you okay?"

He called to the nurse.

She attempted to focus. She saw a blurred Gerald sitting in the corner of the room with Terry standing right next to her. She must've been dreaming.

The nurse came running into the room and adjusted a tube that was attached to her arm giving her a sharp pain in the crease of the immobilized limb.

Gerald rose out of the chair and stood next to Terry.

"You both can have ten minutes with her." The nurse started walking out of the room. "But no more," she said sternly as she shut the door behind her.

"Hey, girl. What's up?" Terry tightly held on to her hand. "Thank goodness you're all right. I have been leaving work early for the last few days to come see you here at the hospital."

Bit by bit things started to come back to her. She slowly began remembering Trent, Hines and Detective Ross and everything that happened. Had it been a dream all along? If so, what was she doing in the hospital?

"Nurse Ratched said we can't stay long, but after I finish some of these women's heads I'll come back." He smiled and squeezed her hand tighter. "I promise."

"Terry?" she whispered. Her voice was dry and it was difficult to speak. "I know you don't work at the hospital or the beauty shop."

He leaned down and kissed her forehead. "I know you know. They told me someone called and I figured it was you." He sighed. "I was trying to save this for later but the reason I don't work at either one of those pathetic jobs is because—are you ready for this? I own my own shop, girlfriend." He bent down and hugged her a little too hard in his excitement. Her sides ached. "I wanted to tell you but I wanted it to be a surprise. I've been there for a couple of months now, but I didn't want to say anything until I got it off the ground. Now I'm making money hand over fist. I only wish I'd done it sooner." He winked. "I gotta go but I'll be back. I'm sure you have a lot to say to Gerry here. He saved your life."

After Terry left, Gerald came over to her. His expression was a little more somber than Terry's had been a few moments earlier.

"I had no idea. I'm sorry." He frowned.

She should've been the one that was sorry. She had accused Gerald of being in on the whole thing. She had thought him capable of murder.

"I didn't know." Tears welled in his eyes and for the first time he showed some sincerity.

"I talked to the police and they told me everything. They told me what Jeremy Culmer a.k.a. Detective Ross did. They also told me about some drug operation Trent ran."

"You didn't know anything about it?"

"Jordan, you have to believe me. I thought he was cutting me in to take over our competitor Axo. I had no idea about the drugs."

She believed him. She had no reason not to. "And what about Charlotte? You knew about her. You knew Trent was playing me and you acted like nothing happened. I thought we were cool."

He looked down. "I know. I feel terrible about that."

"And what about him setting me up as his alibi? Did you know about that?"

"I had no knowledge of any of that. I just knew he was cheating on you with Charlotte. I tried to be his friend by acting like it was cool to do that, but I really wanted to tell you."

How high school was that? He wanted to be his friend? She felt sorry for him.

"It's okay, Gerald. I feel bad myself. I thought you were in on the whole thing. I even tried to set you against Trent, hoping you would tell me everything."

He laughed. "Is that why you told me you knew everything in the office that night?"

She grinned at the recollection of that moment. "Yup. That's exactly why I said that."

"Oh, that was good. I thought you were talking about the Axo takeover. I was afraid you'd found out somehow and would go back and tell Trent. He would've naturally thought it was me who told. I was scared to death."

"Gerald? What did Terry mean when he said that you saved me?"

"They said you probably wouldn't remember. The night you were in the office with Jeremy, Detective Ross, whatever, I was there, too, only you both didn't know it."

She looked at him inquisitively. "What were you doing there?"

"I was cleaning out my desk. I was getting the hell outta dodge. I came down to the copy room and I saw you in the office with Trent but I couldn't hear you guys. As I said before, I thought you knew everything and were about to tell Trent. He would naturally assume it was me that let the cat outta the bag."

"You were that scared of him?"

"I knew he wasn't a force to be reckoned with. I found out things about him. Bad things. I knew he had some shit going on, but I had no idea to what extent."

Jordan attempted to adjust her pillow. Her back ached.

Gerald reached down and fluffed the pillows for her and then continued. "I heard someone else come up to you guys in the office. He was being very sly about it. I didn't know who it was until he turned around and then I recognized him. You and Trent were still arguing and hadn't seen him yet."

"You knew Detect... I mean Jeremy?"

"I didn't really know him and I didn't remember his name. Trent mentioned him on occasion and I had seen a picture of him before. He told me he used to be married to Jacquie and that they all had owned a business together until Trent ran off with the business and his wife. That's what the 'C' is in PHC Industries. Hines was in on

t, too. He initiated Jeremy's departure. Trent used to laugh when
he told that story."

Jordan did remember Jeremy saying something of the sort that
night.

"Anyway, I was just about to roll out with my belongings when I
heard a shot. I had no idea what to do so I hid behind a desk and
watched the rest."

"So you saw everything?"

"Saw and heard everything in the end." He wiped the sweat off
his forehead. He appeared nervous.

"By this time, I was close enough to hear it all. He told you he
had murdered Hines and Jacquie and then I saw Trent slumped
over in his chair. I figured that was the shot I had heard earlier. I
knew he was going to frame you for it."

"What happened next?"

"You started fighting with him."

She did remember that.

"But you were unable to get away. He almost hung you."

She thought hard for a moment but it made her head ache. She
only slightly remembered that part.

"I had already called the police but they weren't there yet. When
he had his back turned, I ran in with a typewriter and knocked him
over the head with it."

"Where is he now?"

"The police have him. They tell me he confessed to everything.
Even if he didn't, I would've stepped up to the plate and told them
what happened."

"And Trent?"

He sorrowfully shook his head. "He didn't make it."

This was all becoming clearer now. Thinking about this whole
thing all over again gave her a pounding sensation in her head. All
she wanted was some rest.

Reading her mind, the nurse popped her head in and dismissed Gerald.

"It's okay, Jordan. The police are going to take care of everything," he said.

When he left the room, she felt as though this would be the perfect time to cry but the tears wouldn't come. She didn't want to cry. She'd done enough of that the past few weeks. She had been through so much but surprisingly she had come out much stronger.

Her mind drifted to Hattie and she realized she'd been right all along. There was nothing that couldn't be fixed.

She closed her eyes and fell into a deep slumber. This was the first peaceful sleep she had had in days.

***

Jordan stepped up on the near empty bus. It had been a while since she had seen the inside of this vehicle. She sat down in her seat and settled comfortably. She couldn't wait until she got her own car. This bus had become more and more raggedy every day.

Not to mention, along with the passengers, this bus carried way too many memories she would've preferred to forget.

It had been a lengthy six months since the death of Hines and less then that since the demise of Trent.

Although she was feeling more at ease, she still had dreadful nightmares about it. Technically she hadn't quit the job but since the owners were no more, she just never went back. She heard it had been sold anyway. Until she found a secure job, she was doing odds and ends at Terry's new shop. Plus, the ring Trent had given her would tide her over for quite some time. This weekend she and Terry were car shopping.

She heard from the police, stating something or other about all the profits of the PHC Industries going to Mrs. Prescott and that the contract was null and void since they found the person who illegally enforced the changes and put him behind bars where he joined a one Jeremy Culmer.

That was an error on their part. Mrs. Prescott had perished months earlier in that car "accident."

She hadn't spoken to Gerald since she had gotten out of the hospital. They both just went their separate ways and that was the way she preferred it. As a matter of fact, she didn't have contact with any of the employees.

In hindsight, there were things that still weren't clear to her. She slowly remembered certain incidents like when Gerald was in the hush-hush meeting with Mrs. Prescott and Hines; and when he had acted so strangely upon seeing them at the restaurant that day. She knew Gerald still had his little secrets. Some things just didn't make sense and at this point it was of no interest to her. The nightmare was over and there was no way she wanted to rehash any of that.

She sat on the bus and stared out the window at the trees swaying in the wind, gently bending their branches in rhythmic formation, first to the right, then to the left in unanimity. It was a beautiful display of splendor. It reminded her of being a child and relishing the cold. It was a sharp cold that could cleanse your soul when inhaled deeply from within. It was winter and the snow sprinkled on the ground coating the earth in a delicate formation softly embracing the hardened asphalt.

"Well, well, well, I haven't seen you in a while."

Jordan turned around in her seat and saw Hattie smiling at her. She was all bundled up in a checkered threadbare wool coat with a matching hat that had one of those little balls on the top. It bobbed every time she moved her head.

"Good morning." Jordan smiled at her.

Believe it or not, she had actually missed this woman.

"You look beautiful, child. I don't know what you've been doing to yourself, but you look more restful."

"I feel much better, thank you." Jordan was actually happy to talk to the woman. Before, Hattie seemed to be a nosy busybody constantly in her business. Now she realized that she was just lonely. In fact, she probably rode this bus all day long to keep in the company of others. Jordan should be lucky she chose her to befriend. Throughout her darkest hour, she had inadvertently given her sound advice.

"Everything okay now?"

Jordan looked up at her, peering down over into her seat.

"Excuse me?"

"Last time I saw you, you were near tears almost every day. I told you that you could fix it, no matter what the problem was. Do you remember?"

"Oh, that?" She smiled. "I fixed it."

The bus stopped and Hattie stood up in the seat to get off.

"Good for you. I won't be around to give any more advice," she added quickly.

Jordan looked up at her in surprise.

"Yep, moving to Florida next week. Good luck to ya." She walked past her and toward the front of the bus.

"Hattie," she yelled to the front of the bus. "Thank you."

Hattie smiled her eminent toothless grin and winked at her one last time. Then she stepped off the bus disappearing like an old magician's trick. That was the last time she ever saw the old woman.

"Thank you, Hattie."

EPILOGUE

Mrs. Prescott lifted the fruity drink to her lips and sipped gingerly. It was delicious. She could have one of these every day.

She looked out past the horizon and drew in the beautiful sunset that overlooked the docile ocean.

She had planned on just visiting the sunny isle of Ibiza but upon vacationing for a few days, she had bought a tiny little villa just outside the main city.

"Excuse me?" A tiny man with a big accent stood over her table. "I want for you to sign for ze drinks."

He put a bill in front of her and she carefully signed.

CHARLOTTE A. PRESCOTT.

She still couldn't get used to her new name.

It had all been so coincidental. All of it except the fact that she'd had her sights set out on the million dollar man since she had started working for him. She knew Trent would hire her on her looks. She also knew her looks could get him into bed and eventually get him to marry her. She had to constantly dodge Jacquie during their illicit affair but other than that, she was golden. After the murder of Hines, Charlotte became a "little birdie" and told Trent that she had overheard Mrs. Prescott threaten Hines. She lied of course but he took the bait hook, line and sinker. All she wanted was for him to have one more reason to leave her. She didn't realize he would actually think she did it. Trent was so sure, too, but when his private investigator found out Jacquie was dead and his theory was wrong, he nearly flipped out almost completely ruining her agenda.

No one suspected a thing, including those ignorant coworkers of hers. Charlotte came in every day with those ugly-looking dresses that made her sick to her stomach. No one knew she had the body of a model under those potato sacks, no one except Trent. When she found out Little Miss Jordan Overton had received a twenty-thousand dollar ring, she had to pick up her pace. What she didn't know was that the ring was strictly for some sort of set-up Trent had planned. Regardless, it had worked out for her. She had slipped in under the radar and secretly married Trent.

Charlotte became Mrs. Trent Prescott two days before his murder.

Of course the police had questioned her, but what could they find? The first Mrs. Prescott was dead and that asshole Hines was long gone. From what she knew, they were killed by someone in their past. Trent had no family to contest the will, so she got it all. She had legitimately married her husband and she didn't kill or set anyone up. That was left to those bozos. She iced the cake by selling the company to the highest bidder and here she was.

Charlotte lifted her glass to the air. "Here's to Jeremy or Detective Ross or whomever." She slowly lowered the drink to her lips and took a sip, savoring every drop. She sat back in her seat and continued to watch the sunset. "Now this is the life. This is now my life."

ABOUT THE AUTHOR

Laurel Handfield is the author of *My Diet Starts Tomorrow.* She currently lives in the Bahamas with her family and is working on her third novel. You can visit her on the web at http://www. laurelhandfieldbooks.com